Penguin Crime Fiction
Editor: Julian Symons
Hanged Man's House

Elizabeth Ferrars was born in Rangoon and arrived in England at the age of three. She was educated at Bedales School, Hampshire, and took a diploma in journalism at London University, but decided to write novels instead of becoming a journalist. She has had about forty crime novels published on both sides of the Atlantic, and many have been translated into foreign languages, including Italian, Japanese, German and French. *Breath of Suspicion* (1974) and *The Small World of Murder* (1976) have both been published in Penguins. Among her latest books are *Drowned Rat* (1975) and *Blood Flies Upwards* (1976).

Elizabeth Ferrars

Hanged Man's House

Penguin Books

Penguin Books Ltd, Harmondsworth,
Middlesex, England
Penguin Books, 625 Madison Avenue,
New York, New York 10022, U.S.A.
Penguin Books Australia Ltd, Ringwood,
Victoria, Australia
Penguin Books Canada Ltd, 2801 John Street,
Markham, Ontario, Canada L3R 1B4
Penguin Books (N.Z.) Ltd, 182–190 Wairau Road,
Auckland 10, New Zealand

First published in Great Britain
by William Collins Sons & Company Ltd in their Crime Club 1974
First published in the United States of America for the Crime Club
by Doubleday & Company, Inc., 1974
Published in Penguin Books 1977

Made and printed in Great Britain
by Richard Clay (The Chaucer Press) Ltd,
Bungay, Suffolk
Set in Linotype Times

Chapter 1

'Those dogs!' Valerie said. 'Whatever's the matter with them?'

'They've been at it all night,' her brother Edmund said. 'On and on. They've been driving me mad.'

'You didn't get much sleep, did you?' she said. 'I thought I heard you get up once or twice after I came out to see if I could help you.'

'I'm sorry if I woke you.' Edmund Hackett sat down at the table. He looked ill and exhausted as he dropped into his chair. He was in his pyjamas and dressing-gown. His face was haggard and his eyes, grey-green behind large, round, gold-rimmed spectacles, were red with tiredness. 'I went on being sick, or thinking I wanted to be sick and not being able to, for most of the night.'

'Why don't you go back to bed?' Valerie asked. 'I'll bring your breakfast up to you.'

'No, it's all right, just give me some coffee. I don't want anything to eat.'

Valerie, wearing a dressing-gown too, poured out the coffee. She looked at Edmund with concern. He was forty and she was seven years younger, but her attitude to him, for as long as she could remember, even in their childhood, had been maternal. He had always seemed to need it. In his work he might be, indeed she was convinced that he was, extremely competent, but outside it he was a man who found the little practicalities of life almost impossible to deal with. His clothes, his papers, the act of remembering where he had put something down, his health, or making important decisions, such as when he should have his hair cut or what thriller he should read next, all presented him with problems which it seemed were impossible for him to solve without Valerie's advice and assistance.

'Have you had any sleep at all?' she asked.

'A bit towards morning,' he answered. 'You're looking a bit peaked yourself. D'you think you're coming down with it too?'

'I shouldn't think so. I feel quite all right. But I didn't get much sleep either. I started thinking, for some reason, and couldn't stop.'

'Thinking about what?'

'Just this and that.' She poured out some coffee for herself. 'Nothing special.'

'But you've had something on your mind for some time, haven't you? The last few weeks. I've noticed.'

Edmund, in fact, noticed most things, although he often seemed so wrapped up in himself. He was very perceptive. It could make him disconcerting to live with.

'Ah well, I sometimes think about the future,' Valerie said. 'Then I start wondering. I sometimes feel as if I don't really know what I'm supposed to be doing with myself. But it's just a mood, it'll go.'

'You don't usually go in for moods.'

There was a trace of complaint in Edmund's voice. Moods were his privilege. So were uncertainties and indecision. Valerie was the one who was supposed never to be at a loss as to what should be done next. And in general she seldom was. In the long term there might be a certain haziness about her view of things, but it did not show, she kept it to herself. She had been living with Edmund for five years now, ever since her husband, Michael Bayne, had died of a fractured skull when he was rock-climbing, and if she had ever had thoughts of doing anything but live with Edmund for the rest of her life, no one had ever guessed at them.

She was a slender woman, fairly tall, with a calm, oval face which was rather expressionless except when her large grey eyes fastened on something, perhaps some other face, or the movement of a pair of hands, or the shape of a shadow on the fields, or of a cloud in the sky, with a look of probing attention, as if there were something of the utmost importance to her to be wrung from the object. But even then, if she became aware that this had been observed, the look was quickly blotted out by an anxious sort of blankness. She seemed to want no one to be given a chance to see into her thoughts. Yet she was known as a friendly woman, even-tempered, unmalicious, reliable in little acts of neighbourliness. Her presence had helped very much to smooth Edmund's way for him when he had come, only a little before she had come to live with him, to his present job as Deputy Director of the Martindale Research Station near the small town of Keyfield.

'Anyway, we'd better get Dr Inglis,' she said as she buttered toast for herself. 'He'll give you something.'

'No,' Edmund said irritably. He hated having the doctor. It always made him feel that there might be something seriously the matter with him. 'It's just this bug that's around. And I'm over the worst of it. Or perhaps it's something I ate. Those chicken livers we had for lunch yesterday. I don't know. It doesn't matter.'

'All the same –'

'No, he'll just shovel some pills into me that'll make me feel worse than I do already. Val, if you're worrying about the future it's because you're bored, isn't it? And we can't have that. We'll have to talk about it some time.'

'There's no need,' she said. 'It's nothing. I don't know why I said anything about it at all.'

'Oh, I've seen it coming for some time,' he said. 'Perhaps it's actually a healthy sign. It may mean you're beginning to get over Michael's death. Like the restlessness that gets into one when one's convalescent after an illness. It's hell in its own way, but still a good sign. We'll talk about it some time. Only not just now, because I feel pretty much in a fog.'

'D'you think you've got a temperature?'

'I'm sure I haven't.'

'I wish you'd go back to bed.'

'Perhaps I will presently. I'll see. This coffee's making me feel better.'

He did not look any better. His face, always a rather muddy colour, this morning was almost grey and his skin seemed to hang on it loosely, sagging under his chin, and making his neck, above the unbuttoned collar of his pyjamas, look old and wrinkled. He had not combed his hair. It had once been the same light brown as Valerie's, but now it was thickly streaked with grey and it was standing up in tufts above his high forehead, tufts which he made look wilder by frequently raking his fingers through them.

'About that meeting last night,' he said, 'how did it go?'

The evening before he and Valerie had intended to go to the monthly meeting of the Botanical Society in Keyfield, but because he had not been feeling well, she had driven off by herself.

'All right,' she said. 'The same as usual.'

'As dull as ever?' But before Valerie could answer, he burst out, 'Those damn dogs! What's got into them? They've been at it since soon after you went out last night.'

'Have they? I heard them when I got back,' she said, 'but I didn't take much notice of them. I thought they'd just taken it into their heads to bark at the car for some reason.'

'I wonder if anything's wrong.'

'Perhaps I'd better go over and see. Perhaps Charles has got this bug, like you, and hasn't got up to let them out. Only that wouldn't account for their keeping it up all night, would it? I'll get dressed and go over.' She got up and started towards the door.

'You could finish your breakfast,' Edmund said.

'But if something's wrong with Charles ...'

'More likely he's gone up to London and for once forgotten to tell us.'

'In that case someone still ought to let the dogs out. I'll run over and make sure.'

She went quickly up to her room.

It was at the back of the house and once inside it she could not hear the barking of the dogs. Edmund's room faced the home of their neighbour, Charles Gair, Director of the Martindale Research Station, which was why Edmund had been disturbed all night. The two houses were separated only by a narrow courtyard. Charles Gair lived in the old Martindale farmhouse, a long, low house of golden-grey stone, most of

8

which had been built in the seventeenth century, while Edmund's house had once been the stable block of the farm, and looked as old as the other, though inside it had been skilfully converted into a pleasant modern house.

This had been done at the same time as the big block of laboratories had been built farther on along the old farm drive and the acres surrounding them divided into experimental plots for soft fruits. From Valerie's window she could see several long strips of red-brown earth, all striped with the shiny green of strawberry plants, a different variety on each plot, with white blossoms covering the plants. But it would not be so very long now before the yearly orgy of strawberries and cream would begin, of deep-freezing and jam-making. That was one of the perquisites of being connected with a research station like the Martindale. Beyond the strawberry beds was a copse of beeches, still with the May-time glitter on their green, and beyond them a low, rounded hillock, covered with rows of black-currant bushes. There was a faultless neatness everywhere, and because there had been rain in the night but the sun was shining now, everything gleamed as if the whole scene had just had its face washed and its hair combed.

While she was getting dressed Valerie heard Edmund come upstairs and go to his room. So he had decided to go back to bed, she thought. That seemed sensible, after the sort of night that he had had. And as it was a Sunday there was no need to telephone anyone at the Martindale to say that he was ill. And very likely he would be able to go back to work tomorrow. He had a way of bouncing up again rapidly after any sort of illness. His digestion was his worst trouble. It was easily upset by any infection that happened to be around, or even by his own emotions. For he was a worrier. He was probably engaged now in trying to work out how he had picked up this particular bout of sickness. That would seem to him important. He might decide that it had come from Hugh Rundell, the Secretary of the research station, who had had an upset and been away from work for a couple of days last week. Or perhaps Edmund would decide that he had been made ill by a slight row that he had had with Charles Gair yesterday morning. For Edmund

9

was much given to analysing himself, exploring the labyrinths of his own repressed aggression.

Putting on jeans, a cotton shirt and sandals, Valerie coiled her hair up quickly and went downstairs.

As she reached the sitting-room she heard the dogs again. The barking was intermittent now, as if they were becoming tired, but when they gave tongue there was an eerie sound of howling in it that sent a little chill through her veins. What had happened? It was not like Charles to go away and forget to ask her and Edmund to look after the animals, to whom he was devoted. And he had been up to London for a few days only last week. Why should he have gone away again so soon?

She went to the kitchen and took the key of Charles's house from the hook where it always hung. Years ago he had asked her to keep the key for him, so that she and Edmund could look after the dogs when Charles went away. Returning to the sitting-room, she had just started towards the door that opened straight out of the room into the courtyard between the two houses when there was a knock at the door.

She opened it. Hugh Rundell stood there. She was surprised to see him, for he lived in Keyfield and did not often come to the Martindale on a Sunday. He was a tall, spare man of about Edmund's age, with shoulders that sagged a little and who nearly always looked tired, though he drove himself at his work with fierce intensity, as if there were really nothing else in the world that mattered. This morning he was in a light grey sweater and grey slacks, as neat as he always was. His face, with its regular features, always well-shaven, looked very neat too. His hair was a dead-looking brown and slicked down close to his head. His weary eyes were light blue and at the moment had a startled, desperate look in them, as if something had happened to him that he could not understand and very nearly could not bear.

'Val, she's written to me again,' he said. 'God damn the woman, she's written *again*!'

Chapter 2

Valerie looked past him at Charles Gair's house, then she looked at Hugh's face. She had to make a decision about priorities. It happened that the dogs were silent just then.

'Well, come in,' she said. 'I've got to pop out in a moment, but come in. You mean Debbie's written?'

'Yes, yes, Debbie.' He wandered to the middle of the room and stood looking round him as if he were in an unfamiliar place, instead of one which he visited sometimes two or three times a week. He moved as if he were lost and as if he felt that if he planted a foot incautiously it might sink into a quagmire. 'Debbie, of course. Where's Edmund?'

'In bed, I think. He's not well.'

'I'm sorry. Yes – ten months and then she writes again, and about nothing. She needn't have done it. I wish she wouldn't. I wish she'd leave me alone. For one thing, it upsets Isobel so much. She cries and cries every time one of the damned letters comes. This one came in the second post yesterday. And I thought she was going to take it all right for once. She was quite calm, almost amused, I thought. But this morning she won't get up and she's started crying and she won't stop. That's why I came out. I felt I couldn't stand it any more. And I think it only makes things worse if I'm about. She turns against me, as if it was all my fault.'

Debbie was the wife who had left Hugh nearly five years ago, soon after Valerie had come to live with Edmund. The two women had known each other slightly and there had been the beginnings of a kind of friendship between them. A curious fact, in its way, for they had had almost nothing in common and Debbie normally had not had much use for other women. Yet it was because of that rudimentary friendship, Valerie thought, that Hugh now confided in her as much as he did. Though he needed sometimes to let out his own bitterness, his deep and unforgiving sense of injury, he could not endure it when this stirred up feelings too antagonistic to his wife in anyone else. He still seemed to feel some obligation to protect her from attack. And there were plenty of people who were ready to attack her. Debbie Rundell had not been popular at the Martindale. She had been an unsettling influence in too many marriages.

Isobel, the Rundells' daughter, was now a difficult seventeen, with the promise of growing into something like her mother's beauty but with her nature still a mystery, varying from day to day from sweetness to sullenness, from a remarkably adult perceptiveness to an adolescent's prickly self-centredness.

Hugh brought an envelope out of his pocket.

'Will you read this letter?' he said. 'I brought it to show you. I want you to tell me why you think she writes like this. What makes her do it? Is it because she isn't really sane?'

'She isn't asking for anything?' Valerie asked, meaning, of course, money.

'No,' Hugh said. 'She never asks for anything. But she must want something. Only what? *What?*' He normally spoke in a low, monotonous tone, over-controlled, but now, on the last word, his voice went loud and harsh. 'Here, read it.'

Valerie glanced at the window. 'I ought to go.'

'Just look at it,' he said urgently.

'It's the dogs,' she said. 'They keep on barking and barking. I'm afraid something's wrong.'

'This won't take a minute.'

She took the letter and sat down in a chair beside the empty fireplace.

As she began to read Hugh roamed about the room, then flung himself down in a chair, facing her. She first studied the envelope. Hugh's address was written on it in the sprawling handwriting that she had come to know because she had seen most of the letters that Debbie had written to him over the years. The postmark was Paris. There were two sheets of paper inside. The letter ran:

Poor, dearest Hugh – I know you hate to get my letters, you must, but sometimes I get the feeling I just have to write to you. I'm sure you'd sooner I dropped out of your life altogether. But if you would, you'd have divorced me, wouldn't you, and married again? I think probably you ought to marry again, and if you want a divorce, of course I'll agree. Not that it matters one way or the other to me. I know I shan't ever want to marry again. I can't stand being tied to anyone and I can't stand living the kind of life people expect of you if you're married. That awful Martindale! The fearful gossip sessions over coffee. The scandals we used to whisper about one another. Perhaps things would have been better for you and me if we'd lived in London or some big town, then people wouldn't have been able to watch every single thing I did and make me feel they all hated me. But you know what I used to feel about all that, so there's no point in my going on and on about it. You're the only man I've ever been really fond of deep down inside. But that wasn't enough, isn't it funny? I can't really explain it. I'm quite happy in my own way now, so if you ever worry about me, don't. Only sometimes I get this feeling of wanting to write to you. Sometimes I think of Isobel too and wonder what she's like. She's almost grown-up, isn't she? I can't imagine it. I always remember her in that awful school uniform she had to wear, but she was such a pretty thing, wasn't she? Is she very pretty still? But I don't really expect you to write and tell me. I'm moving on from here on Friday, going back to the States, where I want to find myself a new apartment, as I got rid of my old one before I came on this trip. But lots of love to you, dear Hugh, even if it's not the sort of love you wanted. Your Debbie.

The address at the head of the letter was a hotel in the Rue Jacob.

Valerie handed it back to Hugh.

'She never tells you anything about herself, does she?' she said.

'No, all I know is that she moves about a good deal,' he said, 'and presumably has a job of some sort, because she doesn't seem to need money. There've certainly been men in her life too. But apart from that and the fact that she can't want me to write back to her, since she never lets me have an address I

13

can write to, I don't know a thing. So why does she have to write to me at all? What does she want?'

'It can't be anything very rational,' Valerie said. 'Perhaps it's something like wanting to see Isobel, but being afraid to come out and say so.'

'Isobel's very bitter against her, you know,' he said. 'I think she almost hates Debbie's memory.'

'Why do you let her see the letters then, if they upset her so?'

He gave a hard little laugh. 'She opened the letter before I got home yesterday. She knows the writing, of course. And as I told you, I thought she was going to take it in her stride for once. She was busy finishing a dress she'd been making and washing her hair and so on to go out for the evening, to a dance or something, with young Haydon, and she just gave me the letter, saying, "Here's something for you," and went on with her own affairs. But this morning she's crying and crying, just as she always did when she was younger.'

'And you think that's because of the letter and not because of anything that happened with Ivor?'

Ivor Haydon was a young geneticist who had recently come to work at the Martindale.

'D'you know, I never thought of that?' Hugh said. 'I took for granted it was the letter.' He paused. 'Yes, it was the letter. She said so. She said she wished Mummy wouldn't go on writing — and she very seldom says "Mummy" now. She generally says "my mother", in a very detached tone of voice. Very grown-up. Saying "Mummy" was a sign she was upset by the letter. Anyway, Haydon wouldn't do anything to upset her so badly. I've not much use for him myself, but he's not bad in his way.'

'Perhaps he just didn't do enough,' Valerie suggested. 'You never know how they'll take things at Isobel's age. The new dress and the hair-do make it sound as if she expected it to be quite an occasion. And if nothing much happened she may have been unbearably disappointed. But I expect you're right, it was the letter.'

Hugh had leant back in his chair, his hands thrust deep into

14

his pockets, his long legs in their perfectly creased trousers stretched out before him. His chin was sunk on his chest.

'Val, tell me something,' he said. 'You've noticed how Debbie never really tells me anything about herself. Would you say she's actually deliberately secretive?'

'Well, yes, I think I would,' Valerie answered.

'Then would you say ...?' He hesitated. 'It's a melodramatic idea, but I can't get it out of my head. Would you say there's a chance she's got herself mixed up in something – call it dubious? A thing she's really afraid of my finding out about. I know she's getting money from somewhere. Well, suppose it's something illegal. Possibly dangerous.'

Valerie took a moment to consider this new idea. 'I hadn't thought of that, Hugh, but now you've suggested it ...' She met his light blue, tired eyes, but found that they were not really looking at her, but through her to something a long way beyond her. 'Have you suspected this for some time, or only since you got this letter?'

'I think I started wondering about it the last time I heard from her,' he said. 'D'you remember, that letter came from Yugoslavia? And just like this one, it really said nothing at all and didn't give me an address to write to. So I started wondering if she'd written out of a – well, a sort of nostalgia for the old days, when things at least were reasonably secure, even if they were dull, and there was no question of worrying about what was going to happen tomorrow, or the day after. Don't you think she might feel like that occasionally? If she'd got mixed up in something exciting but rather dangerous, don't you think she might have attacks of wishing she was out of it and back in dreary old Keyfield?'

'Would you have her back if she wanted to come?' Valerie asked.

'Good God, no!'

'Are you sure?'

'As sure as I am of anything.'

She doubted it, even if he thought that he was telling the truth. She saw how tense his long body was and how carefully he was handling himself to maintain the appearance of composure. It was always very important to Hugh to appear to be in perfect control of himself.

Keeping his voice deliberately low and level, he went on, 'I'm only trying to find an explanation of these letters of hers. For my own peace of mind. If I felt I understood them, I think perhaps I could discuss them with Isobel, which might help her quite a bit, don't you think?'

'You feel it might help her to have it suggested that her mother's taken up smuggling or spying or something?'

He gave another dry little laugh. 'You think that wasn't a very good idea of mine. But leaving Isobel out, what about this possibility that Debbie's gone in for crime?'

'Well, I never knew her very well, you know. She left quite soon after I got here. You ought to be able to judge far better than I can how far she'd be likely to go.'

'To any lengths, if she felt like it,' he answered. 'She's got a lot of courage and no conscience at all. That's an explosive mixture. It could take her anywhere.'

Valerie was watching his self-contained face, wondering why, in spite of his regular, well-formed features, he was really not in the least handsome.

'I know I've said it before,' she said, 'but I've often wondered how the two of you ever got teamed up.'

'You don't have to wonder why I found her attractive, do you?' he asked. 'My God, I've never known anyone like her! What she saw in me, well, that's a puzzle, though it didn't occur to me at the time. I saw myself as a very desirable husband. There's no doubt about it, I was complacent and perfectly ready to take everything for granted. Now I don't know how I ever managed it. But I think one day she must have thought suddenly she ought to give marriage a try, and I was more of a marrying type than most of the men she knew. And, after all, it lasted twelve years, so she must have got something out of it she wanted. Isobel, perhaps.'

'In that letter she mentions divorce.'

'And in the last one too, d'you remember? But she never comes right out and asks for it. And by now I don't care one way or the other. When she left me, I wanted it at once. I wanted to get even with her. I even thought of hiring a private detective to find her for me and get the thing moving. I remember talking that over with Charles and asking if he knew of anyone I could go to. He knows such an odd collection of people. Then one of her letters came and I began to think ...' He closed his eyes for a moment. Opening them again, he drew his feet in and gave both his knees a sharp slap. 'But I wouldn't have her back now for anything in the world. Because I'd know she could do it again, you see. Any morning when she went out shopping, or to have coffee with someone some morning, she might decide not to come back. And one might not be able to survive a thing like that a second time.'

Valerie was not sure that he had survived the first time. Something that had been in him when she had known him first, a certain vitality and air of wholeness, had died a quiet death. By now she could hardly remember what it had been.

'Anyway, if you were me,' he said, standing up, 'you wouldn't try to talk the thing over with Isobel. I suppose that's what I really came to ask you about.'

'Oh, how should I know, Hugh?' she said. 'What I think I'd do is let her keep her feelings to herself, if she wants to, and grow out of them in her own way. You can't force the confidence of anyone of her age. It's one of the prickliest times of one's life.' She stood up too and as she did so became aware of the key that she had clasped in her hand. 'Those dogs!' she said. 'I'd forgotten them. I must go.'

Just then Edmund appeared in the doorway. He was still in his dressing-gown, had neither shaved nor combed his hair and looked white and shaky.

'I've just been sick again ...' he began, then he saw Hugh. 'Oh, Hugh, I didn't know you were here. I'm sorry to come in like this, but I've had a horrible night. More or less what you had last week, I believe.'

'Then I sympathize,' Hugh said. 'I felt like death. But it doesn't last long. A couple of days and you'll feel reasonably all right. Old Inglis gave me some antibiotic that seemed to settle it.'

'Edmund doesn't want me to phone him,' Valerie said. 'I think it's stupid of him.'

'All right, get him, if you want to,' Edmund said. 'I don't care. I just came down to ask if you've been over to see Charles. The dogs are still making a row.'

'I was just going,' Valerie said. 'But Hugh's had another letter from Debbie that he wanted to show me.'

'Here,' Hugh said, thrusting the letter out to Edmund. 'Read it and tell me what you think of it.'

Valerie left them, hurrying now, suddenly assailed by a sharp anxiety. Suppose something really was wrong in the other house. Suppose Charles had had an accident, fallen downstairs, had a heart attack . . .

She crossed the courtyard which once had been the farmyard where there would have been a manure heap and chickens would have roamed, but which now was paved and had a long, narrow rosebed down the middle of it. A few early roses were in bloom, pink and red in the still, Sunday morning sunshine. The light was very clear and bright. It brought out the golden tinge in the grey stone of the old buildings and made the silvery slates of the steep roofs almost iridescent. The air was full of birdsong and the scents of early summer, freshly mown grass, warm earth, rosemary, honeysuckle. There was not even the smallest white puff of cloud in the sky.

The clamour of the dogs suddenly rose in volume as Valerie crossed the courtyard. Skirting the rosebed, she went to the door and touched the doorbell. She heard it ringing inside and heard a high whine from one of the dogs, then a thud as one of them hurled its heavy body against the door. Valerie rang once more and as there were still no answering footsteps inside, put the key into the door and pushed it open.

The dogs, both Labradors, rushed out at her, nearly knocking her over. They circled her wildly, then rushed back into the house. She took a few steps forward into the hall. It was dark at all times, with only a small window in the three foot thick wall and black beams in the ceiling. Now, after the brightness outside, it seemed to be all in shadow.

'Charles!' she called.

The dogs yelped and whined.

'Charles!' she called again. 'Are you there?'

Her anxiety, which had been only half-real till then, oppressed her with the sudden certainty that some disaster had happened in the house, so silent except for the frenzy of the dogs.

What the disaster was she discovered as soon as she took a few steps forward to the door of the sitting-room and opened it. Straight and still there, black against the blue square of the french window opposite, the body of Charles Gair hung from one of the beams that supported the low ceiling. He was suspended by some kind of cord looped around his neck and over the beam. His feet dangled a couple of feet from the floor. It looked, of all incredible things, as if Charles Gair had hanged himself.

Incredible to Valerie, because of all the people she knew, Charles was the one who she would have felt most certain found the greatest satisfaction in the life he led.

But of course, he had tried to kill himself once before ...

You had to remember that.

Chapter 3

For some seconds Valerie stood staring at the hanged man with that devouring gaze of hers, as if she were trying to draw into herself every detail of the scene before her. Then all of a sudden she turned and went blundering through the shadows of the hall, nearly falling over one of the dogs that were circling round her, and out into the courtyard. The sunlight blinded her. She put both hands to her eyes, pressing her fingers against her eyeballs, and stood there, swaying.

It was five years since she had seen a dead face. That other one had belonged to her husband, Michael, in an Austrian hospital. She had seen no sign of the injury that had killed him. He had looked what the nuns in the hospital had called wonderfully peaceful.

Those had not seemed the right words to Valerie. She had felt that he looked merely aloof, withdrawn. But then, she had always felt that his rock-climbing had been a way of withdrawing from her, of escaping into some secret world of his own. So there had been some resentment in her grief, a wondering anger that he should so often have taken his life in his hands, as he had, as if it had been all his own to waste.

These memories came surging over her as she stood with the warmth of the sunshine on her skin, a chill in her blood and her fingers covering her eyes, trying to blot out the vision of the face that she had just seen, and which no one, even those kind Austrian nuns, by any stretch of the imagination could have called peaceful.

She heard footsteps and felt a hand on her shoulder.

'Val, what is it?'

Hugh had followed her from the other house.

She tried to say the word, 'Charles'. But her throat seemed to have swollen, so that nothing would come out.

He went past her into the house. The dogs had grown quiet except for low whining noises of bewilderment and fear. Valerie heard Hugh's footsteps go firmly across the hall, then stop abruptly. She drew a long breath and went back into the house. Like the dogs, she was suffering from bewilderment and fear, and something special, she realized, had been bewildering her from the moment when she had entered the house for the first time. But what it was escaped her. Standing in the hall, she tried, as she let out that long-held breath, to clear away the fog that was making her stupid.

As she drew in her next breath, she knew what it was that had been troubling her. There was a smell of burning in the house.

It was not the smell of flames, clawing at wood or cloth. It was the smell of charred food, the smell, perhaps, of a saucepan that had burnt dry.

She went quickly into the kitchen. It was a long, narrow place with a sloping roof, in what was the very oldest part of the house. But it was all a shining white now, except for the orange curtains, the copper pans hanging from hooks on the wall, the black and white linoleum tiles on the floor. And it had every kind of modern convenience built into it, a refrigerator, a dishwasher, an electric cooker with an eye-level oven. And it was from the oven that the smell of burning was coming.

She crossed the room. The oven switch was at 300°. She turned it off, then opened the oven door. Inside was a casserole, a heavy iron one, enamelled in bright orange. Putting on an asbestos glove that hung near the stove, she lifted the casserole out of the oven and carried it to the sink. When she lifted the lid, she saw what looked like the remains of a chicken, all blackened and dry, of onions too and what might have been tomatoes sticking to the sides of the casserole. Their characteristic odours were still recognizable in the unpleasant stench.

'What are you doing in here?'

Hugh had heard her come to the kitchen and had followed her.

'Look at this,' she said, showing him what was in the casserole.

He made a face. She put the lid back on the casserole and opened a window to let out the smell of burning.

'I'll show you something else,' Hugh said. 'Come along.'

They had both often been in the house and knew their way about it. He led her to the dining-room. Charles Gair had always complained that it was too small for him to entertain in properly, though this was expected of him as Director of the research station. The room had panelled walls, a big, open fireplace in which an electric heater took the place of the logs that would once have burned there, a narrow table and a set of what Charles had claimed were genuine Hepplewhite chairs. He had always liked to extol his possessions to other people. If the coffee-pot out of which he was pouring their coffee were a Georgian one, they were not allowed to think that he had bought it at Harrods. And when he had last laid his table, whenever that had been, he had brought out some of his choicer possessions, the place-mats and napkins of Cyprus lace, the Waterford wineglasses, the Meissen china. There were roses, charmingly arranged, in a silver bowl. The table was laid for two.

'That's strange, isn't it?' Valerie said.

'*Strange!*' Hugh exclaimed, as if he found the word hopelessly inadequate.

'I mean, to cook a dinner, lay a table like that, and then suddenly go and kill yourself.'

'Perhaps she didn't come.' There was almost a note of mockery in Hugh's voice. 'Or perhaps her husband did.'

It grated harshly on Valerie's nerves. She knew that Hugh and Charles had never liked one another and for all the years that they had worked together had merely endured one another because, as employees of a Research Council, neither had had any chance of dislodging the other from his job, even by complicated intrigue. But with Charles's body hanging in the other room, so hopelessly the loser in any conflict that there had been between them, it was not the time for irony or for what

Valerie thought that she had detected in Hugh's voice, a sound of satisfaction.

But that must have been imagination, for Hugh was not a callous man. He was generally easily moved by the troubles of others.

Yet he stood there, looking at the dining-table that had not been used, with a queer tightness about his lips that was almost a grin.

'We ought to telephone,' Valerie said. 'The doctor. Inglis. Charles always went to him.'

'My dear, he's been dead for hours,' Hugh said. 'It's the police we've got to send for.'

The telephone was in the hall. Mercifully, to call the police there was no need to go back into the sitting-room, a room which, until now, Valerie had always thought of as one of the pleasantest she knew. It was furnished with bookcases, a grand piano, comfortable chairs and some glowing pictures, painted by Charles himself. It had a french window that opened into his cherished garden, where he had made a notable rockery, covered in rare plants, and a lily-pond, and where all the shrubs were perfectly pruned. He had been a man of varied talents and a perfectionist in all things. And he had been an excellent host. Valerie had had some good times in that room.

Hugh put a hand on her shoulder. 'I'll give them a call and wait for them. But there's no need for you to stay here and Edmund ought to know what's happened.'

She hesitated in the hall.

'Did Charles do it himself, Hugh? That table and the burnt chicken – he can't have been thinking of taking his life when he did all that. But he did try once before, didn't he?'

'When Rhona left him.' The quirk of Hugh's lips was definitely a grin now, though not a mirthful one. 'We aren't lucky in our marriages at the Martindale, are we? How could we be, cooped up together as we are. Edmund was the sensible one, staying a bachelor. Go and tell him about this now.'

He was picking up the telephone as Valerie went out into the courtyard.

She found Edmund, still in his dressing-gown, standing in the doorway, waiting for her.

'What's happened?' he asked. 'What's the matter? Where's Hugh?'

She went past him into the house and sat down abruptly on the sofa. All the strength had suddenly gone out of her. She began to tremble.

'Charles has hanged himself,' she said. 'Or he's been hanged. Or . . .' But she could not think of another possibility. She was conscious only of a haze of uncertainty. It was a feeling almost that she could not really have seen what she had. 'He's dead,' she said. 'He's hanging from one of the beams in the sitting-room.'

Edmund said the obvious '*Charles?*' in a tone of incredulity, and looked as if he were about to start denying the possibility of what she had said. But the words did not form, and all at once, with nervous clumsiness, he began to clear the table of the breakfast things, trotting backwards and forwards to the kitchen, carrying one plate or cup and saucer at a time. It was just like him to do something so senseless at such a time.

'Leave it, leave it!' Valerie cried. 'But you ought to get dressed. The police will be coming. They'll want to talk to you.'

'Why me?' he asked, picking up the toast rack between his thumb and forefinger and trotting out to the kitchen with it.

'You're Deputy Director, aren't you?' Valerie replied when he came back. 'They're sure to want to talk to you. Do go and get dressed.'

'*Charles!*' Edmund repeated. 'The man who seemed to have discovered the secret of living. I can't think of anyone I know who got as much out of life as he did. Yet he tried to kill himself once before, of course. And they generally try again, don't they? Or so I've been told.'

'That's what Hugh and I were talking about, and it's what everyone's going to say.' Valerie had her elbows on her knees and was holding her head in her hands. She had started to think of Michael once more, who had trifled with his life again and again, which surely must have meant that he had been more than half-willing to lose it. Certainly her own terrors at the risks he had taken had meant nothing to him, unless he had been actually titillated by them. In some ways their marriage had not been a very happy one. Each had struggled against the peculiar web in which their need for one another had entangled them, quarrelling frequently, finding reconciliation in passion, and never quite speaking the same language. Yet when Michael had been killed, his loss had left Valerie only half-alive.

Charles had been very good to her at that time. He had had a singular gift for conveying a kind of sympathy, of tenderness, that had been almost a way of making love to her, yet which had never made her fear involvement in what she could not have borne just then. Later, when she had come to know him better, she had realized that this was his normal approach to most women, though generally there was no sign of the kind of discretion that he had used with her. He had been a man always pursued by a fantastic amount of gossip, a good deal of which had certainly been true.

And this in spite of the fact that at first sight there had been nothing obviously attractive about him. He had been a small man, wiry and lean. He had had wide shoulders, long arms, a flat nose and a long upper lip, which had given him a distinctly simian character. His skin had been deeply tanned, for he had spent a great deal of his time walking about the research station, working in his own garden and exercising his dogs. His hair, which had been tightly crinkled, had been almost of the same brown as his skin, and this had given him the look of a kind of furriness. His eyes had been brown too, and only his very white teeth, showing in his sardonic smile, had been in flashing contrast with the rest.

It had been his vitality that had drawn people to him, even when they were inclined to think that they disliked him. He had almost always been in quick motion, or talking in a swift torrent of words, and throwing himself into each of his different activities with total concentration. Then all of a sudden he would be relaxed, receptive, calm. And he had been extremely intelligent and had never treated other people as if they were fools. Really it had been deeply important to him to impress them and it was the people with whom he had failed that he had disliked. Like Hugh, for instance.

Valerie heard Edmund go upstairs. A few minutes later he came down again. He had put on trousers and a pullover, had combed his hair and scraped a razor over his face. It had been a careless job and there were still uneven patches of bristle on his jaws.

He went to the door and started out across the courtyard.

Protectively, as usual, she called after him, 'You don't have to go over there, Edmund. You can wait for the police here. Perhaps they won't want you at once.'

He went on.

She got up and followed him.

He went into Charles's house and went straight to the sitting-room. The dogs, who were fond of him and felt reassured by his arrival, came nuzzling at his knees. Edmund stood quite still in the sitting-room doorway, looking in. What had happened to Hugh, Valerie wondered. There was no sound of him in the house. Could he be in the sitting-room? Could he be waiting in there, silently keeping Charles company? Or had he found being alone in the house with Charles rather more than he could bear and had he gone out into the garden?

Suddenly his footsteps came pounding up the stairs from the cellar into the kitchen and he came bursting out of the kitchen as if he were pursued by fiends.

'There's another one!' he cried.

Edmund, still looking into the sitting-room, said, 'Another . . . ?'

'Dead body. Corpse. A man.' Hugh grasped the door-posts of the kitchen doorway to support himself and stood there, wheezing for breath.

'*Hanging?*' Edmund asked.

'No, no, in a cupboard. In the cellar. All cobwebs and dirt.'

'I think I'm going to be sick again,' Edmund said and made a dart for the front door.

But outside in the sunshine, he only stood with both hands to his throat, retching. Valerie, who had not even begun to

26

take in what Hugh had said, gave him a glazed look, refusing comprehension. You did not keep dead bodies in cupboards.

After a moment Edmund came back into the house.

'Sorry,' he said, stroking his bristly chin, looking at Hugh, who had stopped panting but whose face was a greenish-white. 'In the cellar?'

Hugh nodded.

'Show me.'

'Well, for God's sake, keep the dogs out.'

Hugh turned back to the door that opened on to the cellar stairs and led the way down.

He had left the light on below. It hung from a short flex in the centre of the ceiling. The bulb was a weak one. Its pale light, merging wanly with the shadows, fell on white-washed walls, a rack filled with wine bottles, some suitcases, a step-ladder, some empty cardboard boxes and other household lumber of the kind that accumulates in cellars. There was also a cupboard with sliding doors built in along one wall. One of the cupboard doors had been slid aside and out of the cupboard looked a face. It was on the floor of the cupboard, lying on one side, a shrunken, brownish, dry face, with cobwebs with a few dead flies trapped in them making a veil over the features.

Edmund gave a little gasp of laughter.

'It isn't real, Hugh,' he said. 'It's some damned kind of waxwork.'

'It's real,' Hugh said.

'It's plastic.' Edmund went closer to the cupboard. He put out a hand to brush the cobwebs away and look more closely at the face.

Hugh said sharply, 'I shouldn't touch anything.'

Edmund let his hand drop but stooped and looked more closely at the veiled brown face.

'You're right,' he said in a low voice. 'It's a man. It's a mummy.'

'No!' Valerie said, still refusing to believe. 'How could Charles have got hold of a mummy?'

'That's what it is, a mummy,' Edward muttered. He

straightened up. He could be very calm when you least expected it. 'Was the cupboard open when you came down here, Hugh, or did you open it?'

'It was just as it is now,' Hugh said. 'Just that bit open. I haven't touched anything.'

'It always used to be locked,' Edmund said. 'It had a padlock on it. I've been down here with Charles, helping him to fetch up bottles for some of his parties. I remember noticing it.'

'There's the padlock,' Valerie said, pointing.

It was on the floor in front of the cupboard with a whole bunch of keys attached to it.

'God Almighty!' Edmund murmured under his breath. 'This thing looks as if it could have been here for years.'

'D'you think Charles knew it was?' Hugh asked.

'He must have,' Edmund said. 'He wouldn't have had a locked cupboard in his house without finding out what was inside it. Besides, he seems to have carried the key to it around.'

'But what did he want with it?'

'Well, you know what a lot of interests he had. Some of them may have been odder than we realized. I wonder how he got hold of it. The man looks oldish and pretty dark-skinned. But perhaps that's just the mummification process. Dark-haired, anyway. And in an ordinary shirt and suit.'

'Hugh, how did you find him?' Valerie asked.

She did not want to go any closer to the dead thing in the cupboard, yet her feeling about it was almost impersonal, it looked so dry, so dehumanized, so unlikely.

'Yes, why did you come down here at all?' Edmund asked.

'I'm not sure,' Hugh answered. 'It was something to do with not being able to stand waiting about doing nothing till the police came. And I'd a feeling there was something queer about the set-up here. So I started wandering about the house. I suppose I was looking for something, a letter from Charles or anything that might help explain what happened to him. I went upstairs. But everything there seemed quite normal. Then I came down here, just before you came over, and saw that thing, just as it is, the door open, the face looking at me. I lost

28

my head and bolted. Let's go back upstairs now, shall we? If you and Val want to go home, I'll hold the fort here.'

'It's all right, we'll stay,' Edmund said.

He started to climb the stairs. Valerie and Hugh followed him and all three of them seemed to feel the same impulse to get out into the fresh air as quickly as possible. There had been no unpleasant smell down in the cellar, not even one of mustiness, for the cellar was very dry and well ventilated, yet it was very good to smell flowers and earth and grass again.

They were standing grouped outside the front door when the police cars arrived.

They stopped in the drive behind Hugh's car, and a man in a light grey suit got out of the front one ahead of the other men who had come with him. Walking towards the house, he introduced himself as Detective-Superintendent Dunn. He was a youngish man, probably in his thirties, though it would not have been impossible for him to be over forty, for there was a certain disparity between the youthfulness of his light walk, his upright carriage, his fresh-coloured and unlined face, and the guarded maturity of his expression. It had about it a rather hard look of experience, of detachment, of not being easy to surprise.

Valerie wondered how unsurprised he would manage to remain when he saw what was in the cellar. A dead man hanging from a beam in his own sitting-room was one thing, perhaps even an everyday thing to a policeman. But a cobwebbed mummy kept in a cupboard in the home of a respected member of a government research service was something quite different.

Chapter 4

However, Valerie found that she would not be there to see how the detective took the discovery of the mummy, for after asking some brief questions, he requested the three of them to go back to the house opposite and wait there until he and his men had had a chance to look over Charles Gair's.

'Certainly,' Edmund said, 'but there's something I'd better tell you before we do go. There are two dead men in that house, Superintendent. We didn't know that when Mr Rundell phoned you. We only discovered the second body a few minutes ago. It's in the cellar. It's – rather curious.'

'Two? In the cellar, you said. I see.' For all the difference that it made to the detective's face or voice, Edmund might have said four or five, a positive massacre.

'I wish I saw too,' Edmund said. 'Well, we'll expect you presently. We'd better take the dogs with us.'

He called them and they followed him obediently.

They were still nervous and restless, but had stopped their whining. In the sitting-room in the other house Edmund sat down on the sofa and stroked them, pulled their ears and talked to them, till they leant trustfully against his legs and let themselves be soothed. Now that he was engrossed in thinking of the problems of the house opposite, he looked less unwell than he had earlier. Valerie cleared away the remains of the breakfast things, stacked them in the dishwasher and set it humming. Hugh stood at the window, watching what was happening in the other house.

After a moment he turned and said to Edmund, 'I've just thought of something. I think I ought to phone Isobel. She didn't expect me to be gone long, and since she's in the state she's in this morning, I don't want to risk anything.'

'Go ahead,' Edmund said and nodded at the telephone.

Hugh picked it up and dialled, then had to wait so long for an answer that he started muttering that it looked as if the wretched girl still hadn't got out of bed. But at last the ringing-tone stopped and he began to speak.

'Isobel – I may not be home for some time. Something's come up ... Yes, a very unfortunate thing, a terrible thing really. It's Charles ... What? ... Yes, I said Charles. He's been found dead ... Yes, dead ... What? ... Now keep calm, Isobel, these things happen ... No, no, certainly not, don't think of coming. You can't help, you'll only get in the way. The police ... Yes, I said the police. Naturally they're here. A sudden death and all that, you know, in fact, probably suicide ... What? ... Now, for God's sake, keep your head. I told you there's nothing you can do ... Yes, he was found hanging ... No!' He suddenly raised his voice to what was almost a shout. 'I tell you, you are *not* to come! Understand? I mean it! But don't expect me back for some time. I'm with Val and Edmund at the moment and I'll get home as soon as I can and tell you everything ... What?'

It sounded as if there were no reply, but only an abrupt cutting of the connection. The dialling tone buzzed in the room.

'She's coming,' Hugh said with resignation. He went back to the window. 'She's always been beyond me. She never takes much notice of what I say. Too much of her mother in her. She says Haydon will bring her over. I wonder what he's doing there in the house this morning. She said nothing about expecting him.'

Valerie had come back from the kitchen.

'It's early for it, but I think we could all do with a drink,' she said. She went to the corner cupboard where the drinks were kept. 'Whisky, Hugh?'

They all had whisky.

Hugh returned to watching the coming and going at the other house.

'They'll be hours over there, I suppose,' he said. 'Keep us here all day, probably.'

'Talking of Ivor,' Valerie said, 'don't you think I may have been right when I suggested the state Isobel's in today is because of something that happened between them last night and he's round there now, trying to make it up with her? Debbie's letter may have nothing to do with it.'

'Perhaps,' Hugh said with a sigh. 'Edmund, what d'you think of Haydon? You probably know him better than I do.'

'Very bright,' Edmund said, his hands still fondling the dogs. 'A future ahead of him, if he doesn't muck it up.'

'Is he likely to muck it up?'

'You never can tell when they're as young as that,' Edmund said. 'He's got ideas of his own. Some real originality, and that's rare, you know. Too many of us live off other people's ideas. But he isn't particularly easy to get on with. He's got a very good opinion of himself and a hell of a temper. He got across Charles pretty badly.'

'Charles wasn't the easiest person in the world to get on with,' Hugh said drily.

'No, but when you're Haydon's age you shouldn't go out of your way to fall out with the boss. It suggests something's wrong with your sense of proportion.'

'You don't think Charles would have given him a job on the permanent staff?'

'Not a hope, unless Haydon changed his ways a good deal.' Ivor Haydon had only a three-year appointment at the Martindale, of which about two years were still to run. 'Personally, I like him,' Edmund went on, 'and I'd have tried to persuade Charles to keep him on, but I never had much influence with him, as you know.'

'Nor had anyone else, that I know of,' Hugh said.

'Not that I think Haydon's going to want to hang on here for long.' The whisky had brought a little colour to Edmund's exhausted-looking face. 'He's too ambitious. He'll either aim at getting into a university, or one of the big industrial firms, where he'll make a lot of money. Actually, he's talked to me of going abroad, America or Australia. He's a restless sort of chap who isn't going to take kindly yet to the idea of settling down for some time.'

'Then perhaps that's what happened last night,' Hugh said

thoughtfully. 'If he talked to Isobel about going away, when she'd got it into her head he cared for her, I suppose she might think it was the end of the world. She's appallingly young, though of course she doesn't know it. It's awful, I look at that girl and think how damnably little I can do for her ...' He drank up most of his whisky. 'I'm sorry. Talking about this sort of thing after what's happened this morning. But one's got to talk about something while one waits. That man in the cupboard – for God's sake, in a *cupboard*! And Charles, I suppose, knowing he was there, and giving his dinner parties, and asking us in for drinks, and going down those cellar steps to fetch up bottles ...'

'Don't!' Valerie cried violently. 'We've all been at those parties.'

There was something about that thought that brought silence.

About a quarter of an hour later Isobel and Ivor Haydon arrived.

Valerie saw them pass the window and went to the door to let them in. She found them both standing with their backs to it, watching what was happening at the other house. Two men were carrying a stretcher into it. Another man, carrying a camera, was standing in the doorway and had to move back to let the others in. At the sight an explosive sob broke from Isobel. Ivor Haydon put an arm round her shoulders and drew her close to him. She wrenched herself away from him.

'I told you – don't!' she said.

The tears that she had shed that morning made her voice sound as if she had a heavy cold.

He shrugged his shoulders. 'I'd just some idea of helping.'

'Well, you can't help – nobody can,' she answered.

She turned. Although she could sometimes look as beautiful as her mother, she was far from doing so just then. Her golden-brown eyes were red-veined and the eyelids were puffy. Her mouth was purplish and swollen, with the corners turned down in a childishly clown-like grimace. There were purplish blotches on her cheekbones. She was a small girl with sloping shoulders, a tiny waist, plump breasts and plump little buttocks that filled out the tight black jeans that she was wearing. Her hair was of almost the same golden-brown as her eyes and hung straight and thick down her back.

Seeing Valerie, she gasped in a sobbing voice, 'It's awful, isn't it? Isn't it too horrible to have happened?' Then perhaps she saw some surprise on Valerie's face at such intensity of feeling at the death of Charles Gair, for she scraped her hair back from her face with both hands in an abrupt, nervous gesture, let them fall and stood there, looking sullen. 'Well, it *is* horrible,' she muttered, as if someone had questioned this. 'To *hang* himself ... Why couldn't he have put his head in the gas oven, for instance? That wouldn't have been so awful. Or taken some pills. Or ...' She paused. 'That's what he did before, isn't it? He took a lot of pills.'

'Isobel,' her father called from inside the house, 'either come in or go away. There's nothing you can do here, so you'd have done far better not to have come, but since you're here, don't stand there gawping at those policemen. Come in and keep quiet. And you, Haydon – ' Hugh turned on the young man as he followed her into the house. 'Couldn't you have kept her away? I'd have thought you'd have the sense to do that.'

'I did my best, but she didn't take kindly to it,' Ivor Haydon answered. 'She doesn't care much for missing any excitement that's going.'

She turned on him, her small fists clenched. 'That's a foul thing to say, a bloody thing to say. I came because I thought my father might need me. But you haven't got to stay around now. I didn't ask you to come.'

'In my blundering way, that's just what I thought you did,' Ivor said. 'I thought I was at least necessary to drive the car to get you here.'

His tone was sardonic, with a wry sort of amusement used to cover some real resentment at the way the world treated him. He was about twenty-four, tall and rather slouching. What was visible of his face, a high, broad forehead, a straight nose with flaring nostrils, large, noticeably observant blue eyes, was strikingly good-looking, but most of the rest of it was concealed by a wispy reddish beard. In the midst of this a faintly crooked mouth gave him a look of habitual irony, which he usually did his best to live up to. His hair was red and curled over his collar. He was dressed in a flame-coloured shirt with a flowing green and white tie and narrow fawn trousers.

Isobel turned away from him with a look of contempt and dropped on to the sofa beside Edmund.

'I did come because I thought I might be able to help,' she said, looking round at her elders as if she half-expected to find them crumpling up for lack of her support.

'That was nice of you,' Edmund said. 'Hugh, can the child be given some whisky? After all, she hasn't heard all of it. There are some more shocks to come.'

'I'd sooner have sherry, if you've got any,' Isobel said. 'I don't like whisky. What other shocks?'

'Do we tell her, Hugh?' Edmund asked as he got up to pour out the sherry.

'I suppose so,' Hugh said dully. 'Go ahead.'

'What is it, Edmund?' Isobel asked, a trace of eagerness appearing on her tear-blotched face, as if Ivor had not been far wrong when he said that she did not care for missing any possible excitement.

'It's just that there's a second dead man in there with Charles,' Edmund said. 'In a cupboard in the cellar. A mummy. At least, that's what we think he is.'

'A *mummy*?' she said in a low, incredulous tone. Then she gave a high, shrill shriek.

Ivor sat down quickly on the sofa, gathered her into his arms and held her close.

She clung to him now, burying her face in his flame-coloured shirt.

The sight made Hugh look both angry and embarrassed. He muttered something and turned away to the window again.

'Here's that policeman coming over now,' he said. 'Superintendent Dunn. I suppose he's going to expect us to help him with his inquiries. Good luck to him. But how the hell does one address him when one's talking to him? As Superintendent or mister or what?'

'A copper friend of mine told me you call everyone over the rank of inspector mister,' Ivor said. He was stroking Isobel's hair with one hand and reaching out to take her glass of sherry from Edmund with the other. 'Like with surgeons, I suppose. A sort of snobbery.'

Edmund went to open the door before the detective reached it. He had another man with him, so tall and square and burly that he made the superintendent look small and delicately built. But there was a quiet vigour about him that hinted at very highly developed muscles. Coming into the room with his brisk, light step, he introduced the big man as Sergeant Farley.

Then the superintendent said, 'That's quite a situation you've got over there.'

Whatever astonishment he might have felt when the situation had first been revealed to him had gone from his face and his voice. He sounded almost casual.

'I'd like your help now,' he said. 'I'm sure there's a great deal you can tell me about Dr Gair, if not about the other man. About him – you may be interested to know we've made a tentative identification. His passport and his airline ticket and various letters are in his pockets. He appears to be a Dr José Barragan from Mexico City. He's fully clothed, by the way, and appears to have died from a heavy blow on the back of his head.' He looked round the room. 'Does that name mean anything to you?'

He was answered by shakes of the head.

'But how long ago did it happen?' Hugh demanded. 'How long has he been stuck there in that cupboard?'

'At the moment we've no idea, except that to go by the date of his ticket, he arrived in this country on the third of May last year,' the detective said. 'A post-mortem may tell us more. Dr Inglis, of course, is in charge of that. The body's been there a good time, I'd say. That cupboard appears to have peculiar properties.'

'And I suppose he might have stayed there for ever,' Edmund observed, 'if something we don't understand yet hadn't happened in that house last night.'

'Last night?' Superintendent Dunn said. 'What makes you say last night, Dr Hackett? Mightn't it have been this morning?'

'It was last night that the dogs started howling,' Edmund said. 'And they howled all night. I was rather unwell and didn't get much sleep and I heard them.'

'I see.'

Edmund and the detective exchanged a long look. Edmund's eyes looked peculiarly owlish behind his big glasses.

'Daddy – ' Isobel said suddenly, sitting up and abruptly disentangling herself from Ivor's protective arms, 'Daddy, one of those letters of Mummy's came from Mexico City. A year – no, longer than that ago. Don't you remember?'

Chapter 5

Patrick Dunn turned quickly to look at Hugh Rundell and for an instant saw sharp annoyance on his face. The man would have liked to deny what his daughter had said and was almost startled into doing so. But he was not a fool. He was unlikely to lie if the truth could be come by too easily.

None of these people here was a fool, Patrick thought. They were an unusually sharp-witted bunch. That man with the shiny spectacles, who looked so haggard and ill and yet so alert and watchful, and Rundell with his tidy, unrevealing features, and the woman with the oddly compelling stare which drew your eyes back to meet it again and again, and the hairy character on the sofa with the girl, and even the girl herself, well aware of the effect of what she had said, all looked as if their IQs were well above average.

As no doubt ought to be the case among a lot of scientists in a research station. And if none of them was involved in what had occurred in the other house, it should actually be a help. But if one of them happened to have committed a murder, he was liable to have a good deal of subtlety to help him keep clear of trouble, an understanding of his position which would save him from making the more obvious sort of blunder.

'Mexico City?' Patrick said to Hugh Rundell. 'Your wife has some connection with it?'

'I don't know what you call a connection,' Hugh answered stiffly. 'I must tell you, she left me nearly five years ago. Sometimes she writes to me, and once, as my daughter said, her letter came from Mexico City. But as I remember the letter, she wrote as if she were merely on a short visit there. I think she was living in the States at the time.'

'Daddy, you've got the letter,' Isobel said and again Patrick saw the flash of annoyance on Hugh Rundell's face. 'It's in the drawer with all the others she's written you.'

'Yes, yes, I expect it is,' Hugh said. 'And you're welcome to see it, Mr Dunn, if it's important.'

'Thank you,' Patrick said. 'We hardly know yet what's going to be important and what isn't. As you've probably realized, it's murder we're investigating. Not only Dr Barragan's, but Dr Gair's. That apparent suicide was a pretty botched affair. Like Dr Barragan, Dr Gair died from a blow on the back of the head, possibly delivered by a heavy poker that we found under a chair, where it may have rolled when the murderer dropped it. Incidentally, Dr Inglis, who's over there, told me that Mrs Gair left her husband about five years ago and that he tried to commit suicide after it happened.'

No one answered and it seemed to Patrick that all the faces around him became noticeably more wooden than they had been a moment before. They were not going to gossip to him, at least not in front of one another. That made his next step plain. He was only uncertain where to begin. Then his gaze met and held that of Valerie Bayne.

'Now, if you don't mind, I'd like to talk to you one at a time,' he said, 'just to make sure I've got things straight. And since you're the one who actually discovered Dr Gair's body, Mrs Bayne, you won't mind if I begin with you. Is there a room we can use for a little while? My men are still busy in the other house, and anyway, you'd probably sooner not go back there.'

'There's my brother's study,' Valerie said.

She led the way from the sitting-room to a small room at the back of the house. It was furnished with bookcases, a large table, some filing cabinets and two or three chairs. Unlike the rest of the house, which was fairly tidy, though it looked lived-in, this room was in a state of overwhelming disorder. Every surface in the room, including a good deal of the floor, was submerged in books and papers. Several of the drawers in the filing cabinets were half-open, with folders and loose papers bulging out of them. The window overlooked a small, pleasant garden, the strawberry plots, the beeches and the hillock beyond them that was covered in blackcurrant bushes.

'I'm sorry about the mess,' Valerie said, 'but I'm not allowed to touch anything in here, except about twice a year. My brother claims to know exactly where everything is and says that if I even flick a duster around he'll never be able to find anything again.'

'I've seen worse,' Patrick said. 'There's generally a system in this sort of thing, if you can understand it.' He picked his way across the room towards the table. 'Would it be fatal if we cleared a bit of space here so that I can make a note or two as we go along?'

Valerie leant across the table and ruthlessly pushed aside some papers covered with odd-looking diagrams. She moved some books from a chair.

'Will that do?'

Then she cleared another chair for the sergeant, then perched on the arm of the one easy-chair in the room, as if she did not expect to be kept there long.

Patrick settled down at the table. He was a tidy man himself. A member of a large family that had inhabited a council house where space had grown more and more constricted as the family had increased, he had taught himself to be very economical with it, as well as with possessions. It had been a way of securing a certain sort of privacy. If you owned next to nothing it could not be despoiled by predatory hordes of younger brothers and sisters, and if what you had was always carefully shut away in drawers and cupboards, if you were careful not to let your life overflow into the lives of others, you could be fairly safe from intrusion.

He had grown up into a man incapable of owning much or hoarding anything. If an object had no obvious and immediate use, he threw it away. At any time he could have packed his life into a couple of suitcases. But what he had was cherished and carefully looked after. His landlady in Keyfield, in whose house he had occupied two rooms for the last two years, thought him the least trouble-making boarder she had ever had. Yet sometimes, when he saw a room such as Edmund

Hackett's, he felt a strange little twinge of envy, of a kind which he never experienced in the rooms of the merely rich. It was as if he felt here the presence of an opulence, an overflowing wealth, simply in terms of mental vitality, that he had never found in himself. And it was typical of the wildness of such a room, he thought, that there should be one object in it that arrested attention, was apart from everything else and gave real pleasure to the eye.

'Nice picture,' he observed, looking at the one that hung over the fireplace.

It was an explosion of colour that fell more or less into the form of a bowl of poppies. There was a great deal of sunlight in the picture and some dramatic shadow.

'It is, isn't it?' Valerie said. 'Charles Gair painted it. He gave it to us.'

'He was a painter too then as well as a scientist?'

'He was all kinds of things. A marvellous cook. A really imaginative gardener. You'll see what I mean if you compare his garden with ours. We just about keep ours going, but we've never made anything exciting of it. And he was a bit of a musician. Sometimes he'd play the piano to himself for hours and rather well too. He was good at anything that meant using his hands. My brother says that in a laboratory he was one of the neatest, most ingenious experimentalists you could find.'

'You knew him well?'

'Pretty well, I suppose.'

'Then you know the real story of that attempted suicide of his when his wife left him. Could you tell me about that?'

She looked reluctant to answer. 'Is that important now? It's ancient history. And his death wasn't suicide, you said so yourself.'

'As you'd guessed before I said it.'

'Yes, well, there was the casserole in the oven that had burnt dry. And the table laid for someone who didn't come. Those aren't preparations you make if you're suddenly going to go and hang yourself.'

'Perhaps someone came, but didn't stay to eat the meal,' Patrick said.

'And there wasn't even a chair near his feet, that he might have stepped off into the air.'

'No. Odd that. Really careless of someone. Now about the real attempt at suicide ... You see, Mrs Bayne, that mummy in the cupboard makes that situation over there distinctly bizarre. So the more I can find out about Dr Gair himself, the more that may help me.'

She looked away from him to the window. There was a slight frown on her forehead, as if she were concentrating on remembering just what had happened all those years ago. Watching her, Patrick realized that she was in her way a very good-looking woman, though he had not noticed this at first. There was a restfulness about her. She had unusual dignity. But remoteness too. He wondered what that covered, too much emotion that had no outlet or a real detachment.

'I didn't know him well at the time,' she said. 'I'd only come to live here a little while before. My husband was killed, rock-climbing, and my brother suggested I might come and live here with him until I got my bearings. Rhona Gair was very nice to me. She used to drop in, or ask me over there, and we'd have coffee together and gossip. I don't really remember her very well. I was too wrapped up in my own troubles to take much notice of what was going on around me. She was very poised, and had a terrific social manner, and loved giving parties. And so did Charles. And except that they were nearly always for the same people, because we're such a closed little circle here, who see too much of each other anyway, they were very good parties. Only she and Charles seemed to think it was amusing if they kept up a sort of verbal sparring all the time. You know what I mean – criticizing each other and insulting each other in a way that's supposed to make everybody laugh and think what fun it all really is. And of course everyone did laugh, because Charles was the boss and didn't like you to forget it, even when he was being fearfully friendly.' She paused. 'That sounds spiteful. I don't mean it like that. I'm really trying to remember what it was like.'

'Yes,' Patrick said. 'Go on.'

'Well, sometimes I used to feel there was something all wrong about it, and I didn't want to laugh at all. You know there can often be something real behind that kind of sparring. The people are letting off steam in front of an audience because that somehow feels safer than doing it when they're alone. I don't think this is just hindsight. It sometimes made me feel awfully embarrassed, because I thought there was some real rancour behind the comedy. But it never occurred to me that Charles and Rhona were anywhere near separating.'

She was talking more freely now, and her gaze had returned to Patrick's. He was careful not to return it too intently, in case she should suddenly retreat.

'Then one day,' she went on, 'my brother and I and several other people were asked over there for drinks before dinner. My brother had had a visiting scientist on his hands that day, someone from Harvard, I think. Charles had handed him on to Edmund to look after, but we were to take him over with us to the Gairs at five o'clock. But when we got to their house there was no sign of Rhona, and Charles was in a very odd and excitable mood, laughing wildly at his own jokes and spilling the drinks when he handed them round. I thought he was a bit drunk, though that wouldn't have been like him. Then he told us all in the gayest way imaginable that Rhona had packed up and left him that afternoon. He told the American that that was why he'd neglected him all day and kept apologizing. The American was one of the stiff, polite kind and didn't know where to look, but the rest of us all produced the laughs we thought were expected of us, and Charles suddenly lost his temper and damned us all to hell and asked what was funny about Rhona leaving him. Then he told the American he'd drive him to the station to catch his train and told the rest of us to get out. Edmund offered to take the American to the station, because it was obvious Charles wasn't in any state to drive, but Charles wouldn't have it, and he and the American set off. And Charles got about half-way to Keyfield, then drove the car smack into a tree and it turned over. The poor American had some cuts and bruises, but they weren't serious, but Charles woke up in a hospital with concussion and some broken ribs and a broken collar-bone. Not nearly as bad as it might have been, actually. He was pretty lucky.'

'But you aren't calling that an attempt at suicide, are you?' Patrick said. 'I suppose there may have been a – well, an unconscious wish to destroy himself ...' He hesitated, disliking what he thought sounded like psychological jargon. 'But I thought you meant something more definite.'

'Oh, I do,' Valerie answered. 'Something absolutely definite. A few days later he somehow got hold of a lot of barbiturates in the hospital and took the lot. Luckily it was discovered in time and he had his stomach pumped out and was given injections and they pulled him round, for which he didn't seem at all grateful. Then presently they sent him home and he's been there alone ever since.'

'Except for Dr Barragan in the cellar.'

She gave an abrupt shudder. Giving Patrick one of her swift, deep looks, she turned her head away again to look out of the window.

'I wonder if mummification was one of Dr Gair's many interests,' Patrick said.

Chapter 6

The big sergeant made a sound that was very like a titter. Patrick gave him a stern look.

He went on, 'Did he have help in the house or manage quite alone?'

'He had help,' Valerie said. 'Mrs Jardine, the wife of one of the gardeners here, who lives in one of the cottages on the estate, comes in to clean every morning. She gives me a couple of afternoons too. And he's had help in his garden lately, because he had a slipped disc or something. But he did his own cooking. I told you, he was a first-class cook and loved doing it. And a month or two after Rhona left him he bought the dogs and he was absolutely devoted to them. It was then that he gave us the key of the house, so that we could let them out and feed them if he went away. And that's how I managed to get in this morning.'

'Did he go away often?'

'Just now and then.'

'Abroad?'

'Sometimes, to scientific meetings and so on. But mainly I think it was to London. He was there only last week and told us he was going and asked us to look after the dogs as usual.'

'But he did occasionally go abroad.'

He could see that the repetition of the word intrigued her.

'Most scientists travel a good deal,' she said. 'Why?'

'Only that we happened on an odd thing in that house. We were looking round and we came on a drawer in that sort of writing table in the sitting-room which was full of foreign coins. Small change, you know, the kind you bring back with you when you've been on a foreign holiday and which the bank won't take off your hands. There was a mixture, Swiss,

45

French, German, American and some Mexican. It looked as if Dr Gair was quite a traveller. On the other hand, we haven't found a passport. Not that we've searched very thoroughly yet. We may still turn it up. It isn't in that writing table, however, where he seems to have kept most of his personal papers.'

The piece of furniture to which he was referring was a Regency *bonheur du jour*, a delicate, very elegant thing with rows of shallow drawers in which the police had found Charles Gair's birth certificate, the insurance papers on his house and belongings, some letters and all the other documents that accumulate in any household.

Valerie thought it over. 'Perhaps his passport's in his room at the Station,' she suggested.

'Perhaps. We'll look, of course. That hoard of foreign coins makes it look as if he went abroad quite a lot.'

'There was some Mexican money, you said.'

Patrick nodded.

'It's very odd,' she said. 'I can't remember his ever talking about going there. In fact, I don't think he ever talked much about his trips abroad. He said those congresses he had to go to bored him. When he went on a holiday he liked to go fishing in Scotland. But still, if he'd been to a place like Mexico – I mean, such an exciting place – you'd think he'd have mentioned it.'

'And you're certain he never did.'

'Quite certain. I'm sure I'd have remembered it if he had, as I do remember Mrs Rundell's letter coming from there. Mr Rundell showed it to us. He was very distressed, as he always is when she writes, and I remember my brother and me taking the dogs for a walk in the evening and agreeing that it was really very cruel of her not to let him alone. It always made him hope she was coming back to him, and she obviously never was.'

Patrick picked up a pencil and began tapping the table with it.

'However much these congresses bored him,' he said, 'he'd have needed a passport to get to them.'

'Yes.'

'Well, perhaps we'll find it still. Now to go back a bit, Mrs Bayne, you told me how Dr Gair tried to kill himself when his wife left him. Yet you've spoken of your own feeling that there was real rancour between them under what you called the comedy. That's a bit contradictory, isn't it?'

'Yes, it is. It just shows how wrong one can be.'

'So you were surprised at his doing it.'

'Very. No, I'm not sure. He was an awfully complex person, you know. And he'd been in a nasty accident and been badly shocked. I think we all accepted the idea that he hadn't been normal when he did it. When he got out of the hospital he didn't seem unduly upset any more. He went straight back to work and he got busy at home, making that rather splendid rockery in his garden, and he painted this picture you like about then and gave it to us because my brother happened to admire it, and he started giving parties again, and I remember thinking that once he'd got used to the idea that Rhona could walk out on him, he didn't really miss her much.'

'I see.' He considered asking her if there had been other women in Gair's life since that time, but decided that it was unlikely that she would give him a truthful answer. But there was a related question that might be worth asking. 'Am I right that Mr Rundell's wife left him about the same time? Dr Inglis mentioned it.'

He could see that she did not want to answer. She had not minded talking freely about Gair, who was dead, but she was unwilling to involve the living.

'I believe so,' she said.

'You hadn't come here yet?' he asked.

'Oh yes, it was after I came. But it's all a fairly long time ago. I don't remember everything exactly. Actually I think Deborah Rundell went away a little while before Rhona Gair.'

'How long before?'

'A week or two.'

'And that was just coincidence?'

'What else could it be?'

He laid the pencil that he had picked up down on the table again and regarded it as if its exact position were of importance.

'It crossed my mind that the two events might have been connected,' he said. 'That perhaps the two of them quarrelled over Dr Gair. Alternatively, that they worked one another up to leaving their husbands. That can happen, you know. Two dissatisfied women, neither of whom would do anything drastic if the other weren't there to egg her on. That's the sort of situation that can sometimes lead to worse crimes than leaving your husband. Were the two of them friends?'

'I don't know. I don't think so. Not particularly.'

She meant, he thought, that they had had no use for one another at all.

'Then I think that's about all for the present,' he said. 'Thank you for being so helpful. You're very observant. Oh, just one thing more ...'

She had been about to rise, but paused, waiting.

'About your own movements last night,' he said. 'I've got to ask you about them. I believe you went out.'

She nodded.

'At what time?'

'About half past six.'

'Had the dogs started to bark already?'

'No, they'd probably have been out with Dr Gair. He generally took them for a walk about then.'

'And where did you go?'

Somewhat to his surprise, he saw on her face an expression that he knew very well, the slightly scared expression of a normally truthful person nerving herself to tell a lie. But the temptation to stick to the truth was too strong for her. She gave a little sigh and relaxed, making a small, uncertain gesture with her hands as if she did not know if she was doing what was best.

'I meant to go to the monthly meeting of the Botanical Society,' she said. 'It meets in St Ethelbert's Hall on the third Saturday of every month. My brother and I usually go to the meetings together. But yesterday he wasn't feeling well. Soon

48

after he came home from the Station at lunchtime he said he was feeling sick and thought it was gastric 'flu and that he'd better go to bed. There's been a bug around for the last week or two, you know. Several people at the Station have been down with it. So I got him a light supper and went off. And then ...' She paused for so long that he nearly prompted her, but after another sharp little sigh she went on, 'I didn't go to the meeting. I don't know why, but I had the feeling I couldn't face it. So I drove out along the Albaston road to the Bell-ringers' Arms and had dinner there. A very good dinner. They're making a thing of their food there now. I think there's a new management.'

'Were you alone?'

'Yes. And that's why they'll remember me. A woman who goes into the bar by herself and has a couple of drinks and then goes to the restaurant and has dinner with wine and brandy afterwards probably doesn't happen to them every day. I was wearing a red suit incidentally. Quite a bright red. I'm sure they'll remember me.'

Patrick contemplated her with curiosity. For the first time it was curiosity about the woman herself, and not simply on account of what she might be able to tell him about Charles Gair and the dead man in the cupboard.

'You minded telling me that, Mrs Bayne,' he observed. 'Why?'

She gave an embarrassed smile. 'Doesn't it seem a rather mad thing to do?'

'Not if you wanted to.'

'And I haven't told my brother.'

'He thinks you were at the meeting?'

'Yes.'

'Well, if I had to make the choice between a good dinner at the Bellringers' Arms and a meeting of the Keyfield Botanical Society, I think I'd take the good dinner any day. But why haven't you told your brother? Surely he wouldn't mind.'

'It would worry him. It's not the sort of thing I normally do. Not nowadays, anyway. My husband and I ... But that was different, of course. Going off like that alone would make my brother think I'm not happy here. That I'm dissatisfied. Restless. And I don't want him to think anything like that. He's been so good to me.'

But it's what you are, Patrick thought, and wondered if she had gone to the Bellringers' Arms in the hope of picking up a man. If so, he could have given her advice on better places to go to.

'What time did you get home?' he asked.

'About a quarter to ten.'

'Were the dogs barking then?'

'Yes, but I didn't take much notice. I thought it was just the noise of the car driving up that set them off.'

'And you didn't notice anything else unusual?'

'No.'

'Then I'd be grateful if you'd ask your brother to come here,' Patrick said. 'And thank you again for being so helpful.'

She stood up and he stood up with her. The sergeant opened the door for her.

In the doorway she hesitated.

'If you haven't got to tell him . . .' she said.

'About your wild night out?' He smiled. 'I'll do my best.'

'Thank you.' Her face was grave, as if it mattered to her. She turned and went out.

The sergeant stretched before he sat down again. He found most chairs too small for him and was generally most comfortable on his feet. He grinned and asked, 'What was she really up to?'

'My guess is, exactly what she said,' Patrick answered. 'As to why, well, we'll see. But you can check her story later.'

'You don't think she was the one who was supposed to have dinner with Gair and did him in instead?'

'It wasn't a woman's crime,' Patrick said. 'Hanging him up by the neck on that bit of clothes-line would take more strength than she's got.'

'But using a blunt instrument on him when he wasn't expecting it wouldn't be beyond her. Then the loyal brother comes along and strings him up to make it look like suicide, and sends her off to the Bellringers' to set up a conspicuous alibi.'

'That's going a bit fast.'

'I'm just thinking aloud, sir. Of course, she might have been the one who was expected to dinner but found him dead already when she got there and lost her head and bolted.'

'And then went and ate a large dinner in public? Don't you think she'd have felt a bit queasy for that? I've found a number of dead bodies in my time and to this day it turns my stomach. To tell the truth, I'm not feeling just at my best at the moment.'

'Well, here comes brother,' the sergeant said, who looked as if he could eat anything, drink anything and find a dead body every day without suffering a twinge of indigestion. 'The man who was on the spot when it happened.'

The door opened and Edmund Hackett came in.

Chapter 7

Edmund walked familiarly through the chaos in the room and sat down in the chair that Valerie had just left. He gave a little grunt as he relaxed in it, as if it were a relief not to have to stand. He still looked ill, with an air of having shrunk inside his clothes. They seemed to hang on him unnaturally loosely. But his voice was normal as he stated, 'You want to ask me if I noticed anything unusual yesterday evening.'

'Yes,' Patrick said, 'that's just what I was about to ask you.'

'Well, I didn't,' Edmund said, 'until the dogs started barking. My sister had left the house about six-thirty to go to a meeting of the Botanical Society in St Ethelbert's Hall. We were to have gone together, but I wasn't feeling well, so she made me a light supper before she left, though I told her I didn't think I could eat anything. She gave me some soup, however, and an omelette and I started it just about as she left me and to begin with it seemed to make me feel better. Then about an hour later I started vomiting. And it was about then, I think, that the dogs started barking.'

'I see,' Patrick said. 'That was about seven-thirty or thereabouts, then.'

'Yes, I should think so.'

'But the noise didn't worry you at the time.'

'I was feeling too damned lousy to worry about anything but myself. I did begin to worry a bit when they kept it up, off and on, all night. But mainly I was irritated at the row. It didn't occur to me that anything had happened to Gair. I suppose again I was thinking too much about myself. It was my sister who suggested he might be ill or have had an accident.'

It amounted to very little. At the same time, Patrick thought, it was oddly glib. The words came easily and it even seemed as if talking were doing Hackett good. His face looked less drawn than when he had come into the room.

'So until the afternoon you'd intended to go out,' Patrick said.

'Yes, with my sister.'

'And Dr Gair knew that?'

'Yes, I should think so. Yes, I'm sure he did.'

'So if he'd wanted to invite someone to the house whom he didn't want you to be able to gossip about, yesterday evening would have been a good time for him to choose.'

Edmund nodded in apparent surprise that he had not thought of this himself. 'Yes, that's quite true.'

'And I suppose a number of other people supposed you and your sister would be going out,' Patrick said.

'You mean if someone – it's the murderer I suppose you're talking about – wanted to come here without being seen by us, he'd have known it was a good time for it. Yes, of course. But that presupposes it was someone within a fairly small circle, who knew our ways pretty well.'

'Did anyone know that you'd decided in fact not to go out?'

'No, I wasn't sure of it myself until after I'd got home and begun to realize how ill I was feeling. But there's something I think I ought to say. I don't spend my whole time looking out of the window. I mean, if I'd been, say, in this room, working, anyone could have come and gone without my seeing them. Or if I'd been in the garden. Gair certainly had plenty of visitors whom my sister and I never saw.'

'Of course. But he couldn't have been sure that you wouldn't see them.'

'No.'

Patrick tapped the table with the pencil again.

'When did you last see Dr Gair alive?' he asked.

'See him or talk to him?' Edmund inquired.

'Did you see him after you last talked to him, then?'

'Yes, the last time I saw him was when he took the dogs out for their usual evening walk. I didn't notice the time, but it was before my sister left the house. She may have seen him too. Probably it was about six o'clock. That's when he usually went out.'

'But you didn't see him come back.'

'No, but he generally stayed out for about an hour. However, as he was expecting a visitor and I suppose had preparations to make for the meal apart from the chicken in the casserole, he may have come home sooner.'

'And the last time you talked to him?'

'That was in the morning. We had a bit of a row, as a matter of fact. Gair was a very easy person to have a row with, though luckily they didn't usually last long.'

'What was this row about?'

'The design of some new greenhouses we're going to build at the Station. We disagreed about the ventilation system.' Edmund looked slightly amused. 'Not really an adequate motive for murder, Superintendent.'

'I wasn't about to suggest that it was,' Patrick answered drily. 'But now I suppose those greenhouses will be built according to your plan.'

'Not necessarily,' Edmund answered, still faintly smiling. 'Because I'm Deputy Director of the Martindale, it doesn't mean that I automatically become Director, now that Gair's dead. In fact, I'd be very surprised if it happened. There's a certain prejudice against internal appointments. I'll have to hold the fort until the new appointment's made and then step down again. And the new Director may be someone I get on less well with than I did with Gair. He was difficult all right and we had our rows, but we really understood each other pretty well.'

Patrick returned Edmund's quizzical look without expression. 'I'm not accusing you of anything, Dr Hackett.'

'No, but I'd be a fool if I didn't realize how easy it'd be to pick me out as the murderer,' Edmund said. 'I was alone here, there was no one to see me come and go, and I had the keys of the house.'

'I haven't even begun to think of picking out a murderer,' Patrick said. 'I'm just trying to find out all I can about the circumstances. For instance, that matter of Dr Barragan. Are you quite sure you never heard his name at any time?'

'Quite sure,' Edmund said.

'Funny thing,' Patrick said, 'I'm not sure of it myself. Seems to me I've heard the name sometime, though I can't remember when. As I told you, to go by his airline ticket, he came over to this country on the third of May last year, and planned to return to Mexico a fortnight later. Did you ever hear Dr Gair speak of going to Mexico?'

Edmund shook his head. 'And if he had, I'm sure I'd have remembered it. It's a place I've always wanted to go to myself. Sounds fascinating. Are you assuming Gair murdered the doctor?'

'I'm not assuming anything yet.' Patrick had unconsciously picked up the pencil again and was tapping the table with it. 'I told Mrs Bayne a curious thing we found in that house. We found a collection of foreign small change from a number of countries, including Mexico, but we can't find a passport. Yet Gair must have had one. You don't happen to know where he might have kept it?'

'I'm sorry, I've no idea.'

'Would he have kept any private papers over at the Station?'

'Perhaps. I can get you the keys if you want them.'

'Thanks. We probably shall.'

There was a pause.

'Is that all?' Edmund asked after a little.

'I think so, for the present.' But Patrick knew that there was still something that he wanted to ask Edmund Hackett before he went away, though for the moment he had lost track of what it was. Suddenly it came back to him. 'The Gairs – they never had a divorce, is that right? Do you know why they didn't?'

'I suppose they couldn't be bothered.'

'Do you know where Mrs Gair lives?'

'In London, I think, but I don't know her address.'

'You haven't seen her yourself since she left?'

'No, there was no reason for us to meet. We weren't particularly friendly.'

'I see. Well, thank you for your help. Would you mind asking Mr Rundell to come in now?'

Edmund got up to go.

As he had for Valerie, Sergeant Farley got up to open the door and when Edmund had gone treated himself to another stretch before perching again on the inadequate chair.

'He's dead right, isn't he, sir?' he said. 'He'd the best opportunity of anybody. He was here alone and he had the keys to the house. And you may yet turn up a motive.'

'But allowing for all that,' Patrick said, 'can you see that man doing anything so stupid as trying to cover up a murder committed by a blow on the head with a fake hanging that wouldn't fool a child? I can see him hating Gair a lot more than he admitted. I can see him turning violent. But I can't see him doing anything downright stupid. None of this bunch is stupid. They aren't the usual mindless yobs we're used to. Well, here comes number three.'

Hugh Rundell seemed more uneasy than either Edmund Hackett or his sister. Patrick noticed the stiff walk, the way the man shuffled his feet before he sat down, the way he crossed and uncrossed his legs.

He started off quickly before Patrick could begin to question him. 'It was a horrible experience finding that man in the cupboard, Mr Dunn. It was horrible finding poor Gair too, but that's – oh God, what am I saying? I was going to say, that was a natural sort of murder. I mean, some kind of row must have flared up between Gair and whoever it was and the man struck out at Gair with that poker and killed him. And then did that thing of trying to make it look like suicide. All normal in its way. But that mummy in the cupboard ...' Though the words tumbled out fast, Hugh's voice remained low and monotonous. 'I found him, you know. Mrs Bayne had come over here to tell her brother about Gair, and while she was gone I took a quick look over the house, more to keep occupied than thinking I'd find anything important, and I found *it* – that man. And I can't think of any explanation except that Gair was quite insane, although none of us suspected it. He was neurotic, he was difficult, he and I hardly ever saw eye to eye about anything, but the thought never crossed my mind for a moment that he was actually mad.'

'I'm certainly beginning to get the impression that he was an unusual man,' Patrick said. 'Had you ever been down in that cellar before, Mr Rundell?'

'Yes, once or twice. But I'd never given the cupboard a thought.'

'Of course, you weren't the first person to go down there yesterday evening,' Patrick went on. 'The murderer went down there. And one thing I'd like to know is whether the murderer discovered what was in the cupboard before or after he killed Gair. In other words, was it because that old murder somehow came to light that he killed Gair, or had it nothing to do with it?'

'He must have suspected something, mustn't he?' Hugh said. 'Or why should he have opened the cupboard at all?'

Patrick nodded. 'Yes, why?'

'And he must have got hold of the key somehow, and it's more likely, isn't it, that he got it off Gair's dead body than that Gair let him have it? Unless ... No, that would have been too crazy, even if Gair was mad.'

'Unless what?' Patrick asked. 'What did you start to say?'

'An absurd thing. Too absurd. I was going to say, unless Gair himself unlocked the cupboard to show the other man the mummy.'

'And was killed for it?'

'Yes. But I don't believe in that for a moment. Please don't take any notice of the idea.'

'It's interesting, all the same. That Gair, for some reason, wanted to show that body to someone. The thought hadn't occurred to me. I'll remember it.'

Hugh had an irrepressible attack of fidgeting, crossing and uncrossing his legs again and digging his hands deep into his pockets and taking them out again.

'No, it's too mad,' he muttered.

'The dead man himself, Dr Barragan,' Patrick said, 'his name doesn't mean anything to you?'

'No.'

'But you had a letter from your wife, from Mexico.'

'Yes, but ...' Hugh jerked himself upright in his chair. 'I've been thinking about that. I've been thinking, suppose my wife and this man knew one another. Suppose they even wanted to marry and he came over here to see if I'd divorce her. Well, he'd have come to me, wouldn't he, not to Gair? Why, if there was any connection between him and my wife, should he have gone to Gair? It doesn't make sense. So I think the fact that the man was a Mexican and that my wife once wrote to me from Mexico must be a coincidence. She's written to me from all over the place. I once had a letter from Yugoslavia. She travels a great deal. Only yesterday I had a letter from her from Paris.'

To Patrick coincidence was a dirty word. Not that coincidences didn't happen all the time. Amazing ones. But if what appeared to be a coincidence cropped up in his line of work, he knew that it was highly dangerous to write it off as one until all other possibilities had been tested out.

'Does your wife write to you often?' he asked.

Hugh shook his head. 'I've had perhaps half a dozen letters from her since she left me.'

'Did she and Mrs Gair know each other well?'

'The two errant wives. Yes, pretty well. We're a fairly intimate little circle here.'

'Were they friends?'

'They detested one another.'

'Do you happen to know Mrs Gair's present address?'

'No, I don't know anything about her. I never saw her after she left Gair and he never spoke of her.'

'I see. Then that's all for the present,' Patrick said, 'except that I must ask you what I'm asking everyone. Where were you yesterday evening from about half past six to midnight?'

As he said it, he had a feeling that he had just missed something. Rundell had been nerving himself to answer some other question, and it had not been asked. At the question as to his whereabouts the evening before he seemed to relax.

'I was at home,' he said.

'With your daughter?'

'No, alone. She went out for the evening with Haydon. That's to say, she went out about seven. And certainly she was home before midnight, though I'm not sure when she got in. But around eleven I heard her running a bath. For most of the evening, however, I was alone. I spent it having two or three drinks, then cooking myself a chop, then watching television for a time – there was a thriller film I wanted to see – then I went on with a thriller I was reading, then I went to bed. And I can't prove any of it.'

'No. Well, it's usually the most law-abiding people who find it hardest to provide an alibi.' But the man had been very ready with his statement, Patrick thought. Almost too ready. He had had it all prepared. But he would have known, of course, that he was bound to be asked where he had been at the time of the murder and he had had plenty of time, waiting in the other room, to think out what to say. And what he had come up with was in fact the hardest kind of alibi to prove a lie. It was so entirely probable. 'And now I'd like a word with your daughter,' Patrick said.

He saw alarm flare in the other man's eyes.

'Is that necessary? She can't know anything that would help you. She hardly knew Gair and she was with Haydon all the evening.'

'All the same,' Patrick said, 'I'd like to talk to her for a few minutes. You can stay here, of course, if you want to.'

Hugh got to his feet. 'No – no, she probably wouldn't like that. She'd think I was interfering. She's very touchy about that at the moment. She's at a difficult age. And I'm not clever at handling it. All right, I'll send her in to you.'

He went out.

Patrick beat a quick little tattoo on the table with the pencil.

'Jim, if you found yourself with a body on your hands,' he said, 'what do you think you'd do with it?'

'Well, I wouldn't put it in a cupboard, that's for sure, sir,' the sergeant said.

'But what would you do?'

'I think if I was one of this bunch, I'd put it in a bath of acid. Must have been quite easy for someone like Gair to lay his hands on the stuff.'

'Quite true.'

'Then again, I might dump it across a railway line.'

'Or else?'

'I might chop it up in the bath and dump it piece by piece in other people's dustbins.'

'You seem to have given the matter a good deal of thought,' Patrick said. 'Yet the fact is that Gair, who I'm sure had a lot more brains than you or me, just stowed that body away in a cupboard. Why?'

Chapter 8

'Well, it seems it was a bit of a peculiar cupboard, doesn't it, sir?' the sergeant said. 'Like those crypts you hear about in some foreign churches, where I believe some bodies haven't decayed for centuries and it's called a miracle, and the dead people are treated as saints, when it's all a question of temperature and ventilation.'

'You don't believe in miracles?'

'No, sir. I'm a rationalist.'

It occurred to Patrick that this was one of the most personal remarks about himself that the big man had ever made to him.

'Saint José Barragan of Keyfield,' Patrick murmured, as if he were experimenting with this title for the dead man, 'who was murdered by Dr Charles Gair a year ago. Or wasn't he? Have we got to look for someone else for that murder? Perhaps the man who did the job last night. But still, there must have been some connection between Gair and Barragan. But what? And what was Barragan doing in this country?'

'Missing Persons may come up with an answer to some of that,' the sergeant suggested.

'Missing Persons!' Patrick exclaimed. 'Of course! That's why I felt I'd heard the name before. He's been on their list for months. I shouldn't have forgotten that. So they'll be able to tell us something about his background. That may help.'

The door opened and Isobel Rundell came in.

She looked as if she were almost looking forward to the coming interview. The marks of tears had nearly faded from her face and there was an air of exhilaration about her, the tautness of a kind of excitement. She looked very much prettier than when Patrick had seen her last. But he did not welcome the change. That kind of brightness could easily be the sign of the pleasure that most accomplished liars take in practising their peculiar art. Sitting down, smiling at him, Isobel might have been making the first challenging move in a complex game of wits.

Not that Patrick was altogether against being told a few lies at the moment. Showing them up for what they were sometimes helped to crack something open. And he was tolerant of the compulsive liar, which was lucky for him, since he had to deal with such people nearly every day of his life. It was the deliberate and calculating lie, told with full understanding of the consequences, that could stir a mood of vengeful violence in him.

'I shan't keep you long, Miss Rundell,' he said. 'I'd just like to know what brought you here this morning.'

'My father did,' she answered. 'He telephoned. He said Dr Gair had been found dead and said something about suicide and that I wasn't to expect him home for some time.'

'So he didn't ask you to come?'

'Well, he did really. He sounded in a pretty fearful state – he gets into a state very easily, though he pretends he doesn't – and I could tell he obviously needed me, so I came.'

'Did you know Dr Gair very well?' Patrick asked.

'Oh no, not *well*. You see, he always thought of me as a child. He didn't realize I'd grown up. So we couldn't communicate. Not that he wasn't always very nice to me, after his fashion. He'd known me since I really was a child, you see, and he'd always given me a box of sweets or something at Christmas, and he went right on doing it without ever thinking I might like something else now. Actually I don't really care for sweets much, because if I'm not very careful, I put on weight. I mean, I never eat potatoes and things. But he really meant to be nice to me and I did appreciate it.'

'That's fine,' Patrick said. 'One likes to know there's some gratitude in the world. Now can you tell me where you were last night from say six-thirty on?'

She gave him a slightly suspicious look, as if she were afraid that he was not taking her as seriously as she thought fit, but his expression was bland.

'I was out with Ivor Haydon,' she said. 'I think I went out about seven o'clock and met him at the Golden Paradise – that's that Chinese restaurant in the High Street, I expect you know it – and we had dinner, then we went to the cinema. We saw that marvellous thing about the Mafia at the Excelsior. And after that I went home and had a bath and went to bed.'

'Dr Haydon saw you home, did he?' Patrick said. 'What time was that?'

She laughed. 'No, I saw *him* home. I was driving, you see. My father wasn't going out, so he said I could have the car, and I love driving when I get the chance, which isn't actually very often, because he won't buy me a car of my own, he says he can't afford it. But that's strictly nonsense. The truth is, he doesn't trust me with a car, whereas I'm a *very* good driver.'

'So you dropped Dr Haydon off at his home,' Patrick said. 'Where is it?'

'He's got digs in Beacon Street – 37 Beacon Street.'

That was only a few minutes' walk from where Patrick lived himself.

'And what time was that?' he asked.

'About half past ten, I think.'

'Now I'd like you to think for a moment, Miss Rundell. Don't answer in a hurry. But you said yourself one of your mother's letters came from Mexico.' He still looked bland, but he was watchful. 'Did you ever hear Dr Gair or anybody else say anything that connected him with Mexico?'

She returned his look thoughtfully and, as he had suggested, took her time to answer. And this was where it would come, he thought, the lie, the story made up out of the whole cloth. Something dramatic and bound to rouse his interest in her. For she had been trying to do this ever since she had come into the room, making a display of her very feminine young body with a blatancy that had its own kind of innocence. And she had been showing a slight fretfulness because Patrick, who was seldom attracted by extreme youth, did not respond to it.

But he was wrong about what she would say. In fact, she said nothing. She only gave a slight shake of her head. He wondered if he had already heard the lie that she had come into the room prepared to tell. Was there something wrong with her story of how she had spent the evening?

'Then I think that's all,' he said. 'Would you ask Dr Haydon to come in?'

'Are you going to question all the people at the Martindale?' she asked. 'Because of course the group of us here this morning are here just by chance.'

'I'll probably get around to them all in time,' he said. 'I've started with you because you happened to be on the spot.'

'Ivor, for instance,' she said. 'He's here this morning only because I asked him to drive me up. He's only been at the Martindale a short time and he hardly knew Dr Gair.'

'Then I shan't have to ask him for much of his time,' Patrick said. 'Thank you, Miss Rundell.'

She looked downcast for a moment, as if she were sorry that the interview was over, then got up and slouched out of the room, the exuberance with which she had come into it evaporated.

The sergeant gave Patrick a rather knowing grin and said, 'You could have handled her differently if you'd felt so inclined. She'd have enjoyed it.'

'And we wouldn't have found out any more than we have,' Patrick replied. 'Now at least we know she doesn't eat potatoes. That was probably true.'

'You didn't believe the rest of it?'

'There was something wrong with it, I don't know what.'

'You may know more when you've talked to Haydon.'

'Oh, he'll confirm what she said, you can count on that.'

'There's one thing strikes me,' Farley said. 'If it's true what she said that she had the car, then Rundell hadn't got it, which would have made it difficult for him to get up here.'

'There are buses. He might even have walked.'

'Five miles each way?'

'It's not impossible. He might even have let her have the car on purpose to give himself an alibi. Better check the buses anyway.'

'About that cupboard, sir ...'

'Not now,' Patrick said. 'Here's Dr Haydon.'

'Doctor this, doctor that,' the sergeant muttered. 'And not a medical man amongst them who could write you a prescription for a stomach ache.'

'Except Dr Barragan, who's past it,' Patrick said. 'Come in, Dr Haydon.'

Ivor Haydon, settling into the same chair as all the others, was the only one among them who showed anything like anger at being questioned. That was how he would approach all authority, Patrick thought. Anyone with the slightest degree of power over the young man would be seen as his enemy. He snapped his answers back at Patrick with an air of tight-lipped resentment and tried to convey the impression, which was certainly false, that he had next to no interest in what had happened to Charles Gair.

But Patrick had been right in saying that Haydon would confirm everything that Isobel Rundell had said. They had met at the Golden Paradise, Ivor said, at about seven-fifteen. He was sure of the time because she had been late and he had been irritated and had kept looking at his watch. Then after dinner they had gone on to see the film at the Excelsior and afterwards Isobel had driven him back to his digs. He had got home, he thought, about half past ten, had played records for a while, then gone to bed.

'And if you're going to ask me am I surprised at someone having murdered Gair,' he went on without being prompted, 'the answer is no, he had it coming to him.'

'You didn't like him,' Patrick observed.

'He was a bastard,' Ivor said. 'Mind you, a brilliant bastard, but a bastard.'

'In any particular way?'

'In every way. Women – well, that was his own business, but I'm not surprised his wife left him. I'm all for freedom, but to be like that at his age ... Then you never knew where you were with him. One day you were his brilliant discovery who'd be an FRS by the time you were thirty, and next day you were a bloody fool who couldn't tell a polysaccharide from a protein. And he didn't like me, and if a person doesn't like me I don't feel any obligation to like him. I didn't lick his boots.

You had to if you wanted to keep in with him. He couldn't have enough flattery. That's why he liked to surround himself with nonentities. There's no one here who really counts, you know. Hackett has his points and if he'd never got dug in in a place like this he might have got somewhere. But he's pretty much gone to seed and that suited Gair. He wouldn't have liked competition.'

'Would you say then that his murder was probably committed by one of his associates?' Patrick asked.

The young man looked startled, then dismayed. A flush appeared on his cheekbones.

'Oh no, I never meant to suggest anything like that. Not at all. I mean, they're a pretty good bunch. Very good to work with. I don't want to give you any wrong ideas about them. I was just telling you my own feelings about Gair. But murder, well, that's different.'

'Murder happened.'

'Yes.' Ivor's bearded face grew thoughtful, as if he were regretting having spoken as freely as he had. He waited a moment, then as Patrick had no more questions for him, got up and left the room.

'And that's that for the present,' Patrick said, standing up too. 'We'd better go back across the way and see if they've turned up anything interesting.'

But little more had been discovered in the other house since he and the sergeant had left it. In particular, a more thorough search had not turned up the missing passport. It worried Patrick more than he entirely understood. Its absence seemed important, though he was not sure why. Had it been lost, stolen or destroyed? Or was it simply in the Director's room at the Station? He decided to look into that next.

Meanwhile a message had come to him from the police station, asking him to ring them as soon as he could. He used Charles Gair's telephone to make the call. He was given some information for which he was half-prepared. As he had thought, Dr José Barragan was well known to Missing Persons in London. He had been one of the most hunted-for men on their list for the past year. He had arrived in England on the

66

third of May, to attend a medical conference, had gone to the hotel in Knightsbridge where he had booked accommodation, had asked them at the information desk to recommend some interesting restaurant for dinner that evening, had had them book him a table there, had gone out but had never arrived at the restaurant and had never been seen again.

And it happened that his son, Alberti, also a doctor, was in England at present. He was working as a post-doctoral fellow in Cambridge. At the news from Keyfield he had been contacted immediately and he was now on his way there to say whether or not the body found in the cupboard in Charles Gair's house was indeed that of his father.

Chapter 9

When the two detectives left for Charles Gair's house, Hugh
said that he and Isobel had better be getting home. Valerie
suggested that they and Ivor should stay for lunch. Not much
of a lunch, she said, but she could open some tins and produce
a meal of sorts. They thanked her but stuck to their decision to
go home.

When they had gone Valerie went to the kitchen, put bread
and cheese on a tray and brought it to the sitting-room.

'I'll cook this evening,' she said as she set the tray down. 'It's
too late to get started now.'

'I couldn't eat anything anyway,' Edmund said, helping himself to another drink. 'My guts have been giving me hell all
the morning. I've been feeling I could be sick again at any
time.'

'I'd eat something all the same,' Valerie said. 'You didn't
have any breakfast.' It was the maternal streak in her showing
itself, the assumption that if you could tempt a person to eat
their troubles must be lessened.

'A bit of starvation won't hurt me,' Edmund said. Sitting
down, he pushed his fingers through his grey-streaked hair,
which made it stand up in more disordered tufts than ever but
seemed to release some of his tension. 'I suppose I ought to be
doing some telephoning around to tell all the others what's
happened, but I don't look forward to it. And I'll have to ring
Speight some time, to tell him he's short of a Director.'

Sir Timothy Speight was Secretary of the Research Council
under whose auspices the Martindale Research Station oper-
ated.

Valerie cut some bread and cheese for herself.

'I wish you'd eat just a little,' she said, and without waiting for Edmund to refuse, cut a second slice of the bread, put it with some cheese on a plate and carried it across to him. 'We're going to have the Press descending on us soon, I imagine. A mummy in a cupboard must have news value. Edmund, did Charles really kill that man, d'you suppose?'

'I'm not supposing anything.' Absent-mindedly, Edmund began to eat. 'I don't want to talk about it. I don't want to think about it. I'd like to pretend none of it ever happened.'

'You don't sound awfully grief-stricken.'

'Are you?'

'I think I'm too shocked to know what I feel. I'm trying to blot it all out because I can't bear to remember what I saw this morning – Charles hanging there, and then that man in the cupboard, with all those cobwebs and the dead flies caught in them ... But grief? I quite liked Charles, I suppose, but he didn't mean much to me. And I don't think he really meant very much to anyone. Isn't it tragic, to have been so enormously talented and to have had all that charm he had, and yet not to have been able to stir up real affection in anybody?'

'It's funny, you know,' Edmund said, 'soon after Rhona left him I got the idea he was falling for you. In a serious way. But you seemed so unaware of him that he got discouraged.'

'I was unaware of most things at that time.' But she considered it. 'No, he was very nice to me, much more understanding than I'd have expected of him once I got to know him better, but that was all.'

'It was all that understanding that made me think it was serious,' Edmund said. 'I wonder where Rhona is now. I suppose the police are going to want to track her down.'

There was a knock at the door.

When Valerie opened it, she found Patrick Dunn there once more.

'I'm sorry to trouble you again so soon,' he said, 'but I'd like to go over Dr Gair's room in the research station. If Dr Hackett will take me over, I'll be grateful.'

'Certainly.' Edmund hurriedly finished the remains of his bread and cheese. 'And you'll be wanting a list of the people who work there, won't you? I can give you that over there.'

He stood up, patting his pockets to make sure that he had his keys, then he and the superintendent walked away together towards the laboratory block.

Valerie discovered that she was hungrier than she had thought and cut some more bread and cheese for herself, then made some coffee. Then she emptied the dishwasher of the things inside it, put in the things that had been used since she had set it going that morning, put a bowl of water down on the floor for the dogs to drink, then pulled on her gardening gloves, thinking that she would do a little weeding. But although she was in a state of extreme restlessness, she found that the thought of any normal activity actually repelled her. Taking the gloves off again, she went back to the sitting-room to stand at the window, looking at the house opposite.

She felt curiously afraid just then of being alone, which was not at all like her. There was a long, low cupboard in the sitting-room at the base of the bookshelves that covered one wall and she caught herself glancing at the closed door with a kind of dread. She knew that all that the cupboard contained were some albums of records, yet she felt a sickening little fear that if she were to open the door, she would find something unspeakably dreadful behind it.

She thought of the cupboard in the other house and then of Charles. The recklessness of the man, she thought. To let her and Edmund have a key to his house when he had had a secret like that inside it.

But of course it had not really been recklessness. Charles had judged their characters correctly. They had never used the key except to go in and look after the dogs. They had done no prying. Charles could have had half a dozen corpses concealed in the house without her or Edmund ever finding it out.

And suppose that was what he had had. Was it possible? Not really any more impossible than that he should have had just one. That by itself was enough to start up all kinds of horrifying speculations. Her imagination gave her a very bad half-hour. She was glad when Edmund returned.

'What were they looking for?' she asked.

'I think anything that might throw light on things,' he

answered. 'But mainly for that passport. They haven't found it. I suggested it might be missing simply because Charles sent it off recently to get a new one and they said they'd look into it. They're still there, going through his papers. I rang for Madeleine and she's there, helping them.' Madeleine Boyd was Charles's secretary, a self-contained young woman of extreme efficiency. 'Now I'm going to do that telephoning around. I'll have to call a staff meeting for tomorrow morning. When I've done it, I thought we might go for a walk. I don't know about you, but I know I'm not going to be able to settle down to anything. And we could take the dogs out.'

'You don't think we'll be wanted here?'

'By the police? Dunn says not for the present. You know, I find that man rather impressive in his way. I'd rather like to know him better.'

The world was full of people whom Edmund thought that he would like to know better than he did, but he seldom had the pertinacity to pursue his desire.

He settled down now beside the telephone with the notebook in which he had the addresses and telephone numbers of all the staff of the Martindale written down. Making the necessary calls took him more than an hour. He tried to be brief, but everyone to whom he spoke wanted to be told the whole story from beginning to end. He told them all that he would tell them everything at tomorrow's staff meeting, but still the questions poured out, usually the same ones, until he lost patience and became so abrupt that it started to sound almost as if he suspected each of his listeners in turn of having some dubious connection with the murder.

Then he tried to ring Sir Timothy Speight, whose home number he did not know and had to obtain from Inquiries, only to be told, when he got through to Lady Speight, that Sir Timothy was away for the week-end, and would not be home until late in the evening. It was five o'clock before it was possible for Edmund and Valerie to start out on their walk.

Valerie had not noticed it happen, but some time during the day the sky had clouded over. The shining morning had been replaced by a grey afternoon. She put on a cardigan and joined Edmund in the courtyard, where he was waiting for her with the dogs. They started off past the new, red brick buildings of the Station and down the old farm drive towards the road. They were silent as they walked along together. They normally spent a good deal of time in one another's company without feeling that they had to talk. When they reached the road, they turned to the left in the direction of Keyfield. There was not much traffic on the road, but Edmund called the dogs to him and put them on their leads. He kept hold of one lead himself and gave the other to Valerie. They went on towards a stile some distance up the road where they would be able to leave it for a path that meandered across the Martindale estate and would finally lead them back to their home. It was a route often taken by Charles Gair when he had taken the dogs out, and which they followed placidly, content to be with Edmund and Valerie, who were old friends and to be trusted.

A little before they reached the stile they came to a small house belonging to a member of the staff of the Martindale, Oswald Fullerton, a biochemist, who worked on the pigmentation of fruits. He was about fifty-five and had been at the Martindale for as long as anyone could remember. He was a short, stolid, unimaginative man, very hardworking, though he had never been known to publish anything except one paper when he had been quite a young man, and he was now quite without ambition. If his wife Myrtle was about, he rarely opened his mouth. They were both of them in their front garden now, Oswald mowing the grass and Myrtle spraying the gravel path to their door with sodium chlorate. She was about the same age as her husband, and, like him, had a square, hard-looking body with muscles well developed by the hours that they worked in their garden. Her hair was grey and cropped short, her face deeply tanned. At a first glance it seemed open and ingenuous, but her small eyes were observant and suspicious and she could be counted on to hand on anything unwarily told to her in confidence at incredible speed and in a dangerously distorted form.

'There you are!' she cried when she saw Edmund and Valerie approaching. It sounded almost as if they had kept her waiting.

'And those poor dogs. What's going to become of them now? They'll have to be destroyed, I suppose, or are you going to keep them? Of course, animals feel much more than people realize. I'd offer to take them ourselves if it weren't for Christabel. You can't expect her to adjust to them at her age, can you?' Christabel was the Fullertons' ancient and domineering cat. They also kept rabbits, which they occasionally ate, budgerigars and geese, and they used to put out saucers of milk in the evenings to encourage the hedgehogs that came snuffling around their garden.

'Come in, do, and have a glass of beer,' Myrtle went on. She brewed her own beer, made dandelion wine, baked her own bread and wove the material for her clothes. 'Ever since Edmund telephoned we've been struck dumb by shock. The things that happen nowadays! Violence everywhere. You can't get away from it. It's because no one leads natural lives any more. Everything out of tins or the deep-freeze and everyone idle and bored when their lives could be so rich and interesting if only they weren't so lazy. But to think of poor Charles being murdered! As I said, we've been struck dumb. Have the police found out anything, d'you think? They were here a little while ago but they only asked questions, they didn't tell us anything. Do they know why it happened?'

'I don't think it happened because he ate things out of tins,' Edmund answered. 'As a matter of fact, he left what would probably have been a very tasty chicken casserole in the oven, but unfortunately it got rather over-cooked.'

Myrtle gave him a wary look but decided not to notice that he might be laughing at her.

'Mucked up stuff,' she said, 'and battery fowls at that. We never touch them. Now you'll come in for some beer, won't you? There's so much we want to ask you.'

Oswald had joined her at the gate.

'I expect Edmund and Valerie have had just about all the questions they can take,' he said. 'But do come in. If you don't want Myrtle's beer, we've some fairly drinkable sherry.'

'I think, if you don't mind, we'll just go on on our walk,' Edmund said. 'It's true it's been a very wearing day.'

'That's just what Charles said yesterday evening!' Myrtle exclaimed. ' "Thank you, Myrtle love," he said, "but I think I'll just be getting home. It's been a very wearing day." '

'Yesterday evening?' Edmund asked quietly.

Myrtle nodded. 'Oh yes. I shouldn't be surprised, from what you told Oswald on the phone, if we were the last people to see Charles alive. And that's what I told the police. He came along here, as he so often did with the dogs, and I asked him in for a drink, but he refused, and then instead of going on to the stile and home by the path, he turned back the way he'd come, as if he was suddenly in a hurry. And just think, if only he'd come in for that drink, he might not have been murdered at all. Because probably, coming home earlier than he usually did, he surprised a prowler or someone. Don't you think that's what happened?'

'You may be right,' Edmund said. 'I'm glad you mentioned it to the police. About what time was it that Charles stopped here?'

'About half past six or quarter to seven, I think,' Myrtle answered. 'I know I was just going in to start cooking dinner when I saw him coming along the road.'

'And all he said was that he'd had a wearing day, he didn't say he was in a hurry to get home because he was expecting somebody?'

'*Was* he expecting somebody?' she asked eagerly. 'A woman, I bet. You didn't say anything about that on the phone.'

'He was expecting someone,' Edmund said. 'He'd laid the table for two. But if it was a woman, she wasn't the one who killed him. At least, it wasn't a woman who strung him up. The police are sure of that.'

'I'm sure it was a woman he was expecting to dinner, all the same,' Myrtle said. 'After all, we knew our Charles, didn't we? It was usually a woman. And I'm fairly sure I can guess who it was, because I've seen them together in Keyfield more than once, and you could tell from his attitude, if you know what I mean, that it was something a bit more than a casual meeting. But that's just surmise, of course, so I'd better not talk about it, anyway to the police. There's nothing I detest like irrespon-

74

sible gossip, as I'm sure you know. We're just riddled with it at the poor old Martindale. But I don't mind telling you who it was, because I know you won't spread it around. It was Isobel Rundell.'

Edmund and Valerie stared at her incredulously.

'*Isobel?*' Edmund said. 'That child? It's impossible.'

'A very precocious, over-sexed child, as you may have noticed,' Myrtle replied. 'I tell you, I've seen them together in the Singing Kettle.'

'He was probably buying her a chocolate sundae,' Edmund said.

She shook her head. 'His attitude to her wasn't fatherly. And even if she is just a schoolgirl, that wouldn't have meant anything to Charles. Anyone over the age of consent on up into middle age was all right with him, just so long as she was willing. And that child's just been crying out to be seduced.'

'Dear, don't you think you're letting your imagination run away with you?' Oswald said in the diffident tone that he often adopted when he spoke to his wife. 'That's just guesswork.'

'I'm very good at guessing,' Myrtle said.

'Only not this time,' Valerie told her. 'Isobel was out for the evening with Ivor Haydon. So really you might be wise not to mention that idea of yours to the police.'

'Haydon?' Myrtle said. 'Hmm.'

The way she said it made Valerie wish immediately that she had said nothing about Isobel and Ivor having been out together the evening before, for God knew what form this piece of information would take when Myrtle handed it on to the next acquaintance she met with.

Having said good-bye to the Fullertons, Valerie and Edmund went on up the road towards the stile.

On the way, Valerie remarked, 'It's extraordinary, isn't it, how some people are allowed to live out their lives without being murdered? The ones who do get murdered aren't always the ones you expect.'

Edmund did not respond. He had retreated into sombre thoughtfulness.

When they had gone a little farther Valerie spoke again.

'There's really no reason to worry about Isobel, you know. It couldn't have been her.'

'No,' he said.

'But you're worrying all the same.'

'Not about that.'

'What is it then?'

Frowning at the ground ahead of him, he looked as if he did not mean to answer. It was as if the words were being dragged out of him against his will when he said, 'Val, it wasn't you Charles was expecting, was it?'

She gave a start and felt colour flood into her cheeks.

'Me?' she said. 'Whatever made you think of that? Of course not.'

He turned his head to look at her searchingly. 'It really wasn't?'

'Edmund, really!'

He raised a hand to run a finger round inside his collar, as if it had suddenly become too tight.

'I was sure it couldn't be you,' he said. 'But you never went to that meeting last night, did you? And you didn't tell me you didn't go.'

'No.' There was still bright colour in her cheeks. 'I'd have told you some time. I just felt at the moment that I – well, I didn't want – '

He raised a hand.

'I'm not interrogating you,' he said. 'If you don't want to talk about it, don't. I just happened to hear you hadn't been at the meeting when I telephoned the Isaacses this afternoon. Sam was out and I talked to Ruth. She said they'd both been at the meeting and had wondered why we weren't there. We, she said – both of us. I told her I'd gone down with that bug and left her thinking you'd stayed at home to look after me, but then I started wondering. And if by any chance it was you Charles was expecting – '

'It wasn't, it wasn't!' Valerie broke in. 'And I've told the police the truth about where I was, so don't worry about that. I'm sorry I didn't get around to telling you about it too, but of course I should have sooner or later. Only the whole thing was something I didn't really want to talk about at all, something I don't quite understand and that I can't really explain –'

'I said, don't talk about it if you don't want to,' he interrupted. 'For God's sake, I know those bloody meetings bore you stiff. You only go to them because I do.'

'It wasn't that.'

They had reached the stile and had paused beside it. The hawthorn hedges to right and left of it were still white with blossoms and the scent of it was strong and a little sickly on the evening air. Valerie leant an elbow on the stile.

'Though perhaps it was,' she went on. 'A kind of boredom, a dissatisfaction with myself. I wanted to go away alone and think. And at the same time I wanted to get out of the rut I've been in lately, and away from domestic things too. So I went to the Bellringers' and had some drinks and a very good dinner and rather enjoyed myself, but failed to do any useful thinking. And now I don't know why I thought that going off like that would help.'

Edmund had also propped himself against the stile. The dogs were puzzled by the pause and tried to wriggle through the stile into the field beyond it where they knew they would be let off their leads again to run at liberty. One of them began to whine softly.

'Of course I've been expecting something like this for some time,' Edmund said. There was distress on his face but his voice was level. 'I think I've told you that. I've seen you getting more and more restless recently. Naturally, because you aren't living as you should. You're wasting yourself. It means a great deal to me, having you to live with me, but it isn't a full-time job for a woman like you. And all those voluntary jobs you tried your hand at and always gave up, they weren't what you were looking for. You'd the makings of a real professional historian before you married, and you probably still have. So why don't you take it up where you left off and see if you can make a new life for yourself?'

'Yes, why?' She gazed out across the plot of raspberries beyond the stile. 'But why did you think I might have visited Charles, Edmund? Why me, of all people?'

He moved uneasily. 'I'm sorry, it was just an unreasonable fear.'

'Yet a real fear,' she said, 'though it seems so unlikely.'

'I don't know,' he answered. 'You see, I was ill, I'd been vomiting, I hadn't my glasses on and I saw her ... By the way, I haven't told the police this, though I half wish I had. But whoever it was may have been just a casual visitor or even someone just pushing a pamphlet in at the door or collecting for cancer research or something, and I didn't see why I should mix them up in the thing when I couldn't even see them properly. But I did see someone coming away from Charles's house about half past seven, though without my glasses I couldn't even be sure if it was a man or a woman. And then this afternoon I heard you'd never been to the Botanical Society meeting, and remembering how Charles seemed to feel about you once and thinking of this restlessness of yours, well, I started working myself up into a crazy panic.'

'Panic that I'd murdered Charles?'

'I don't know. No, of course not. Just panic that you'd get involved.'

She laid a hand over his. 'You can't have been thinking very clearly,' she said. 'I know you're as blind as a bat without your glasses, but you aren't colour-blind. If you'd seen me coming away from Charles's wearing the red suit I had on yesterday evening, you'd have recognized that, wouldn't you? Was this person you saw dressed in red?'

Chapter 10

Edmund blinked at her, then he laughed.

'No,' he said. 'In some neutral colour. It might have been a raincoat. But I'd quite forgotten you were wearing your red suit. That's just the kind of thing I do forget. I never notice what people are wearing.'

'All the same, if you'd seen me there in red, you'd probably have remembered it,' Valerie said. 'So now you can stop looking at me so doubtfully and be sure it really and truly wasn't me you saw come out of Charles's house yesterday evening.'

'I didn't see her come out,' he said. 'I only saw her come away from the house. She may never have got in. She or he. We're almost as bad as Myrtle, aren't we, assuming it must have been a woman?'

'Well, it probably was.' Valerie started to climb the stile, then sat down on the top of it. 'Edmund, I want you to understand that the way I went off yesterday evening doesn't mean I'm unhappy, living as we do. And I'm deeply grateful –'

'For God's sake!' he broke in. 'Don't talk about that. I've probably got more out of our living together than you have.'

'But I *am* grateful,' she said, 'and for once I want to say it. I'm not sure what would have happened to me when Michael died if you hadn't stood by.'

'You'd have survived all right. It might even have been better for you if I hadn't been there. If you'd had to get back into a job straight away, like a pilot who's sent up in a plane straight after he's had a crash, you might be happier now. I'm the one who wouldn't be. And if you leave I'll miss you horribly, but I still think you probably ought to go. And not just to some odd teaching job in an out-of-the-way place like this. Go back to university, take up where you left off, get post-graduate training, get an MA, aim at something good. You've got it in you.'

'If I leave, perhaps you'll marry,' she suggested. 'I've never understood why you didn't. It isn't as if you didn't care for women.'

'I've cared too much for too many in my time,' he answered with a touch of uneasy flippancy. 'Do you remember, your best friend Kathleen Jevons, and your second-best friend Joanna Stacey, and that wonderful girl you detested, Miriam Someone, and so on, each breaking a little bit off my heart till there wasn't much left of it and it began to feel very restful to live with my sister. I don't think I'm really made for marriage. But you might marry again if you went away. Have you thought of that?'

'Of course I've thought of it,' she said. 'But it isn't a thing one can plan for, is it? And I'm not sure I'm made for the job any more than you are. The sort of men who attract me in the way that Michael did aren't the kind I can manage to be particularly happy with. It's strange, isn't it? They aren't the ones I can talk to, as I can to you. Just like Michael, they tend to be the kind who are dead scared of any show of affection except when they're actually making love to one. And somehow I almost hate them for that, because of all the things in me that it bottles up. I seem to want something I simply can't have. So I think your idea of my going back to university is the best one for me. But this isn't the time to talk about it. Talking about oneself at all just at the moment seems a bit inappropriate.'

'Oh, I don't know. Life goes on, doesn't it?' Edmund sounded as if his thoughts had gone some distance away from her while she had been talking. 'After all, we aren't involved ourselves and the less we brood on the whole business, the better for us. The police will tell us if there's anything we can do. If I were you, I'd get on and make inquiries about that post-graduate training. I shouldn't put it off. You're getting older, like the rest of us. Now let's get home. There may have been developments.'

Valerie noticed a certain discrepancy between this interest in possible new developments and a desire not to get involved. And as she climbed down from the stile and Edmund followed her and they took the path across the raspberry plot towards home, she was worried by their talk. She could not quite believe that he had imagined that she might have been Charles's expected guest. Even though Edmund was short-sighted and had been without his glasses, and even if he had forgotten that she had been wearing red, she did not believe that he could have failed to recognize her across the fairly narrow courtyard if she had really been there. Something, say, about the way she walked would have been familiar, and she thought that he must know this. But she could think of no reason why he should suggest that the figure he had seen might have been her if he did not believe it.

For a moment she wondered if he had actually seen anyone or had made the whole incident up. Or was he trying to create an atmosphere of doubt about who had come out of the house because he knew perfectly well who it had been? That was the sort of thing of which he was not incapable. He could be quite devious. Had he been trying out on her, rehearsing, so to speak, the story of his uncertainty about the visitor's identity so as to bring it out with more conviction when occasion required? But why? To protect somebody? To give himself a chance to make some quiet little investigation of his own before taking anyone else into his confidence? That was just the sort of thing that Edmund might do. And it might be very dangerous. She hoped that he was not playing any game of that kind, positively encouraging Charles's murderer to turn his attention to him.

They reached home to find that the police cars had left at last. But a car that Valerie did not recognize, with no one in it, was in the drive. However, Charles's door, which had stood open all day, was shut and none of the windows was open. Her imagination, over-stimulated by the events of the day, gave the pleasant old house a frighteningly tomb-like air, darkly silent and secretive.

'Do you suppose the next Director will live in that house?' she asked as Edmund fitted his key into their own front door.

'Or will the thought of that mummified Mexican be too much for him?'

'It's an unusually nice house,' Edmund said. 'I should think he could fumigate the ghosts.'

'Who do you think it will be?' she went on as she followed him indoors. 'Is it likely to be you?'

'I doubt it. And even if the job was offered to me, I'm not sure I'd accept it. I've enough administration on my hands already. A job that got rid of some of that and gave me a chance to get a bit more research done is what I'd welcome, but that isn't likely to come along ... Who's that?' He asked the question sharply, looking out of the door that Valerie had not yet closed at a man who had just appeared round the corner of Charles Gair's house and was standing looking round him uncertainly. 'Anyone you know?'

'No,' Valerie said.

'Oh God, I hope it isn't the Press already.'

The stranger was looking across the courtyard at them with an air of hesitation. Then, as if he had suddenly made up his mind, he came walking towards them with heavy, deliberate strides. He was a young man, black-haired, olive-skinned, short but well built, with strong, rather heavy features and dark, singularly bright eyes. He was dressed in a light fawn suit with an unbuttoned waterproof over it.

'I beg your pardon, you are Dr Hackett?' he asked with a faint foreign accent.

'Yes,' Edmund answered.

'My name is Dr Alberti Barragan,' the young man said. 'I am told it was you who discovered the body of my father.'

'Come in,' Edmund said.

The young man stepped into the room. The dogs prowled around him uneasily and one of them growled until Edmund told him to be quiet.

Edmund introduced Valerie. 'My sister, Mrs Bayne.'

The Mexican gave a little bow. 'I am sorry to intrude on you,' he said. 'I came to see the place where my father's body was found. The police told me where to come. And they told me it was you who found him.'

'That isn't strictly accurate,' Edmund said. 'He was actually discovered by Mr Rundell, the Secretary of this research station. But we saw the body almost immediately after that. It *is* the body of your father, is it? You've seen him?'

The young man nodded. His heavy features were stern.

'Yes, I have made a formal identification. But the condition of the body, his presence here, the whole situation, are beyond my understanding.'

'Won't you take your coat off and sit down?' Valerie said. 'We'll tell you what we can, but we don't understand much ourselves.'

Alberti Barragan slipped off his waterproof and let Edmund take it from him. He also accepted the drink that Edmund offered him.

Holding the glass and sitting very stiffly, he went on, 'You know my father has been missing for a year. I have been in this country for six months as a post-doctoral fellow at Cambridge. One of my reasons for coming was the hope that I might find some trace of my father. But till now nothing has been known of him since he walked out of his hotel in Knightsbridge to go to a restaurant called Neville's, in Uphall Street, where he never arrived. And now, after a year, he is discovered in this fantastic fashion. It is beyond my comprehension. I never heard him speak of any Dr Gair. I never heard him mention Keyfield or the Martindale Research Station. His interests were all medical, he had none in agriculture. There appears to have been no imaginable reason why he should have come here. Yet today his body is found mummified in that cupboard in that house there. I am stunned with shock. I cannot believe it. Yet I must believe it because I have seen him with my own eyes. Yet I still feel what has happened is impossible.'

'As a doctor yourself, perhaps you can at least understand the condition of his body,' Edmund said. 'You can guess how that came about.'

Alberti Barragan shrugged. 'Such a thing is not unknown,' he said. 'It has happened before. I have talked with the doctor who is about to perform the autopsy. That house there is an old one. It has many draughts. And the cellar is a cool place and there is a current of air through the cupboard which de-hydrated the body instead of decomposing it. About that there is no mystery. But how my father came to be in that house is a complete mystery to me. And what he could have done to make anyone wish to murder him is as much a mystery. Was he killed there, or was he taken there dead? Did this Dr Gair wish to experiment with the properties of his terrible cupboard? Did he somehow meet my father by chance and choose him as a victim because he knew my father was a stranger in this coun-try with no friends who would miss him immediately? Tell me, was this Dr Gair such a monster? You knew him. Could that be the explanation?'

Edmund and Valerie exchanged glances. Both of them hesitated.

Then Edmund said, 'Since this morning, Dr Barragan, we both feel we never knew Dr Gair at all. But there's at least a possibility that your father did have some connection with him at some time. The police found some Mexican coins in a drawer in a writing table in Dr Gair's sitting-room, which sug-gests he may have travelled in Mexico.'

'Those coins may have come from my father's pockets,' the young doctor said. 'However, the police told me that no money appeared to have been removed from his body. There was small change, English and Mexican, in his pockets, and there were notes and travellers' cheques in his wallet. So perhaps it is true that Dr Gair once travelled in Mexico. But even if he did, I will swear my father never made any mention of him to any of us in our family. The meeting, if there was one, cannot have been of any importance.'

'Unless, just possibly, your father had a reason for keeping it secret,' Edmund suggested.

'My father was not a man to have secrets,' Alberti Barragan answered. 'He was a good man. His life was an open book.'

'Dr Barragan, I don't know if it means anything,' Valerie said, 'I mean, if there's any connection, but there used to be someone else living here in Keyfield who was in Mexico at

84

least once. Deborah Rundell, the wife of Mr Rundell, who we told you actually discovered your father's body in the cupboard, left her husband about five years ago, but still occasionally writes to him, and one of her letters came from Mexico.'

Alberti Barragan shifted his intense gaze from Edmund's face to Valerie's.

'I am not sure what you are suggesting,' he said.

'Nor am I,' she answered. 'Unless – is it possible? – your father and Mrs Rundell had some sort of relationship and it was that that brought him here. Perhaps he wanted to meet her husband – though of course that wouldn't explain how he got to Dr Gair's house instead.'

'You are suggesting my father and this woman were in love, that he wanted to meet her husband to arrange a divorce.'

'Something like that,' Valerie agreed.

'You do not understand!' the young man said violently. His dark face crimsoned with anger. 'My father was a good man. He adored my mother. He always wrote a letter to her every day if he was away from her. It was when the letters from England did not come that we became anxious. And when a whole ten days had gone by I wrote for my mother to the Chairman of the conference my father had been to attend. And he made inquiries and it became apparent my father had never attended the conference at all. So next we went to our police and they took up our inquiry with the police in London. Besides all that,' he added abruptly, 'my father was a Catholic, he would not have contemplated divorce.'

'No, I'm sorry, I didn't mean to distress you,' Valerie said. 'It's only that three people, your father and Dr Gair and Mrs Rundell, all had a connection with Mexico. So I've been juggling those pieces around in my mind, like a Chinese puzzle, seeing if there was any way I could fit them together. And that was one of the ways. But if you say it's impossible, well, that's that.'

'I think it is quite impossible, truly,' Alberti Barragan said gravely. 'But could you fit your pieces together like this? This lady, Mrs Rundell, and Dr Gair were in love with one another and after she left her husband they met from time to time in different places, one time in Mexico. And there Dr Gair met my father casually, too casually for my father to think of mentioning it at home. But nevertheless, meeting one another casually again in London, that first evening when my father was there, Dr Gair conceived a great fear of the scandal my father could spread about him and decided to murder him. Is that not possible?'

'After what's happened today,' Edmund said, 'I'm inclined to think almost anything is possible. But there's one thing against your theory, Dr Barragan. Dr Gair hadn't the very faintest fear of scandal. In fact, he enjoyed it. If Mrs Rundell had left her husband and come to live openly with Dr Gair, with her husband living only a few miles away, I think Dr Gair would have got a tremendous kick out of it. Of course, a generation ago he'd have lost his job through it, but probably not now. He'd have looked the world in the face with a knowing sort of smile he had and dared it to criticize him. But I can think of another possibility ...'

'Yes?' Alberti Barragan said as Edmund paused.

'Suppose you're half right,' Edmund said. 'Suppose Dr Gair and Mrs Rundell met in Mexico and your father was aware that that meeting had taken place. But suppose the purpose of it had nothing to do with sex. Suppose they were involved together in something definitely criminal. Just guessing, something to do with drugs. Marihuana, for instance. And suppose your father, with his medical connections, somehow found out about it, and then, on his very first evening in England, ran into Dr Gair again, mightn't he have threatened to disclose what he knew to the authorities? Or mightn't Dr Gair have feared that he would? Does that seem to you more likely than my sister's suggestion?'

With a deep frown on his sombre face, Alberti Barragan thought it over, gazing down at the drink in his hand.

'Very much more likely, Dr Hackett,' he said. 'If my father had somehow discovered that Dr Gair was engaged in the drug traffic, he would have gone to the authorities at once. He had a horror of it. He believed it was a worse crime than murder, destroying men and women and even children alive instead of merely taking their lives. Yes, what you have said seems to me very possible. I am grateful for the suggestion. Perhaps it will help us to bring some meaning into this nightmare. Now I must go. I should like you, if you would, to give me Mr Rundell's address, so that I can call on him and ask him about how he discovered my father's body.'

Edmund gave him Hugh's address in Keyfield and the young man wrote it down in a notebook. Then he finished his drink and stood up.

'I must thank you for your helpfulness and apologize again for intruding on you,' he said in his stiffly formal way. 'I will not rest now till the riddle of my father's death has been solved. Who killed Dr Gair, that is no concern of mine, unless it sheds light on the death of my father. But I have told the police here I will stay as long as they desire. Of course, they asked me what I was doing yesterday evening, as was their duty, and I have told them I was at my lodgings in Cambridge, alone, studying. I have no alibi. I could have driven here in two hours, as I have today, and back again without anyone knowing. I have told them also that if I had found Dr Gair had killed my father I would have readily killed him with my own hands. I loved my father. And I love my mother, who is heartbroken, and only a shadow of the woman she was a year ago. When the mystery is solved I shall return to Mexico, to try to help her face our tragedy. Again, I thank you for listening to me.'

He picked up his waterproof and making one of his small bows to Valerie and another to Edmund, left them.

As he walked away towards his car, Edmund stood in the doorway, looking after him.

'I wonder if I've hit on something like the truth, more or less by accident,' he said. 'Charles and Debbie in some racket together and Barragan finding it out ... I think I'll suggest that to our Mr Dunn.'

'He's probably thought of it already,' Valerie said, picking up the used glasses to take them out to the kitchen. 'I've a feeling he's the kind of person who generally thinks of things like that a little before one gets around to them oneself. Now I'd better get on with some cooking, or we'll have nothing to eat this evening.'

Chapter 11

About the time that Valerie's thoughts had gone briefly to Patrick Dunn, he was thinking of her. But he was doing his best not to do so. He considered it was a singularly fruitless way of occupying his mind. Speaking to him as freely as she had that morning meant that she felt a certain confidence in him as a policeman, but not that she felt any interest in him as a man. So it would be the height of stupidity to let his feeling that she might be interesting as a woman distract him from what he ought to be thinking about.

He was far from certain why she lingered in his thoughts as she did. She had been at the back of his mind all day, although it was only after he had got home to his lodgings in the evening and was alone there that he began to find it important to exorcize her image. Yet she was not an outstandingly good-looking woman. There was a certain charm about her calm face, but he had known better and not been moved by them. She had been courteous to him, as all the rest of them whom he had interviewed that morning had been too, but there had been nothing personal, nothing that you could even call friendliness about her manner. He was an official to her, and to people like her officials were a necessary evil on whom society depended if life was to be organized with any comfort, but you forgot their faces as soon as they went out of the room.

So why couldn't he forget hers, since all that she was to him was a witness in a somewhat odd case? But that intent gaze of hers, followed so often by that startled look of withdrawal, acted on him, whether he wanted it or not, as a kind of challenge.

He wondered what she would be like if she could be tempted

to give herself away without fear. And why was she so afraid? Fear of some hurt being renewed, he supposed, either memories of the loss of her husband or perhaps of something in their relationship that had done her an injury. But he himself was hardly the person to set about healing her. He thought of himself as clumsy in human relations, and knew that his work had made him harder and cruder than perhaps he might have been if he had been differently educated.

Yet he had never wanted to be differently educated. He had followed a path in life that he had chosen for himself, against the wishes of his parents who had hoped that he would shed some lustre on the family by going to a university. They had wanted a student son and would have settled for long hair and a beard and dirty jeans if he had brought them the honour of a degree.

But instead he had chosen to be a crop-headed, uniformed copper, a figure of whom, though they had never said it to him, but living in the world that they did, they had been slightly ashamed. And even to this day, when he was no longer in uniform and had risen remarkably fast to a rank which they had never dreamt a son of theirs would be capable of achieving, he sensed a certain embarrassment in their attitude towards him. It was as if, from their point of view, he had gone over to the wrong side and it was only out of their love for him that they tried never to let him see this. But one of his brothers, who had been in frequent trouble for doing shady things with the wrecks of old cars, re-selling them in a condition that made them a serious danger to the public, was really less of a stranger to the rest of his family than Patrick was.

On getting back to his rooms that evening, he had taken off his jacket, had poured out a glass of beer and settled in the one comfortable arm-chair in the room. He had had an early supper of a chop, tomatoes and chips in a café in the High Street before returning home. His room was sparsely furnished, because that was how he liked it. He had managed to persuade his landlady to remove everything from it that was not strictly essential. His only private property in it was the long bookcase and the books in it.

They were mainly history and economics, because it was through them, rather than through psychology, that he hoped to gain some understanding of the human race. Psychology opened too many doors upon darkness. But history might tell him whether he was living in an age unique for violence and meaningless bestiality, or whether people had always been the same. By now he was inclined to believe that they had always been the same and would never be any different. There were also a good many paperback thrillers in the bookcase, of the kind that told a story as preposterously remote from his own plodding hard day's work as he could find, and there was also some poetry, the romantics, nothing modern, because he liked the flavour of them on his tongue and found something mysteriously calming in them, even when he was only half paying attention to their meaning.

That day, after the dramatic business of the discovery of the mummy in the cupboard, together with the hanged body of the Director of the Martindale Research Station, there had been a good deal of plodding hard work to be done, the usual sort of routine stuff. Using the list of names and addresses supplied to him by Edmund Hackett, Patrick and Farley had been round the members of the staff of the research station, asking each when he had last seen Dr Gair, and if they had noticed anything peculiar in his behaviour recently, and if he had ever heard of a Dr Barragan, and so on. The only answer of any interest that he had been given, but which had not seemed very important, was by Mrs Fullerton, who had seen Charles Gair out with his two dogs not long before his death. The rest had only helped to add detail to the picture of Charles Gair that Patrick had already been given. They had all described Gair as a man of notable brilliance, though some had thought that if perhaps he had had fewer talents he might have achieved more in some one direction. And they had all confirmed the story of the strange party after Gair's wife had left him, of the car accident that had followed it and of Gair's attempted suicide in the hospital. On the whole, Patrick had ended up knowing no more than he had when he had finished questioning the people who had been on the spot in the morning.

Then Dr Alberti Barragan had arrived by car from Cambridge.

He had wept bitter tears when he had seen his father, had raged and then had grown ominously calm. His luminous dark eyes had grown hard with a look of purpose. Patrick tried to think of ways in which the young man could have discovered that his father's body had been in Charles Gair's cupboard, for if he had found it out, Patrick believed, he would not have hesitated to kill. Of all the people whom Patrick had interviewed that day, Alberti Barragan was the easiest to imagine as a murderer. But nothing was known at the moment to connect him with Gair or with the Martindale or Keyfield.

There had been an interview too, of course, with the Chief Constable, who had viewed Dr José Barragan's body with ghoulish interest, recalling that famous case up in the Midlands about ten years ago when something of the same sort had occurred, though it had not been a murder, and commenting on how fortunate Dr Gair had been, since it appeared that he had been murderously inclined, to have such a remarkable cupboard in his house.

Then Farley had produced a report of the alibis that he had checked so far.

Mrs Bayne had been at the Bellringers' Arms at the time that she had stated. No one had been found who knew how Dr Hackett or Mr Rundell had spent the evening. But Isobel Rundell and Ivor Haydon had lied about how they had spent theirs. They had not been in the Chinese restaurant, the Golden Paradise. They had been there a week before and on a number of other occasions, but not last night. And Ivor Haydon's landlady had said that he had not been out all the evening. She had heard his record-player going almost uninterruptedly from about seven o'clock until midnight, and if he had not stopped it then, she had said, she would have complained in the interest of her other lodgers. But asked if he had had a young lady with him in his room, she had at first been indignant at this aspersion on the respectability of her house and then had admitted that it was not impossible. With all that music so unnecessarily loud, as the young liked to have it nowadays, she might not have heard anyone come and go. Patrick and Farley agreed that probably the Rundell girl had been there and that she and Haydon had lied about it the next morning out of fear of her father finding out. All of which added up to very little.

It was not particularly helpful either that the only finger-prints on the poker found under the chair in Gair's sitting-room were Gair's own. It looked as if he must have snatched it up to defend himself. The rest of the room was almost free of prints, even of Gair's, but that was not surprising, for Mrs Jardine, his daily help, had given it a thorough polishing in the morning before the murder.

Yet there were certain things bobbing about in Patrick's mind, disconnected and formless, which seemed to him might be of some interest if only he could pin them down. A thought concerning that cupboard in Gair's house. The question of how he had discovered its properties. The house was a very old one. The cupboard had probably been there for centuries. But had it ever housed a dead body before? People didn't normally stuff dead bodies into cupboards.

Normally, no. But suppose you had a reason for doing it, and so discovered by accident what the strange cupboard could do.

Patrick poured himself out some more beer.

Some of these disconnected thoughts were beginning to fit together into something like a pattern.

Next morning he and Farley met at the police station, then drove together to the Martindale. Patrick wanted to hear what answer Ivor Haydon would give when the alibi he had given the day before was challenged. The two detectives entered the building at the main door and Patrick asked the elderly porter in the small office labelled 'Inquiries' where he could find Dr Haydon. The porter answered that Dr Haydon was at present in a staff meeting and was not available. However, when Patrick said that he and the sergeant were police, the porter agreed to see if he could call Dr Haydon out of the meeting, directing them meanwhile to his laboratory, which was up the stairs ahead of them, then along the corridor to the left. They would find a door with his name on it, the porter said.

They went up the stairs, Patrick noticing a smell of chemicals everywhere that made him think of a hospital, and some very abstract paintings on the walls, which he found somehow surprising until he remembered that Charles Gair had been almost as interested in art as he had been in science.

Through doors as they passed they saw benches littered with glass apparatus, and one or two massive instruments, some with moving parts and flickering lights, others solid and white, not unlike refrigerators. It intrigued Patrick that in an institution dedicated to agricultural research there was not a plant to be seen.

In Haydon's room there were two sinks in a bench, a desk, a blackboard with some mysterious scrawls on it, a couple of stools, a microscope table, and a litter of glassware on the bench and of papers on the desk.

They had to wait for some minutes before Ivor Haydon appeared. He came in looking flushed and combative, as if he were prepared to be attacked.

Patrick went straight to the point. 'Good morning, Dr Haydon. About that statement of yours about how you spent Saturday evening, have you any wish to revise it?'

Ivor's crooked mouth, in the midst of the wispy reddish beard surrounding it, quirked up more than usual at one side.

'That's a nice way of saying you think I lied to you, isn't it?' he said. 'Why can't you say what you mean?'

'I said exactly what I meant,' Patrick answered. 'I meant, do you want to revise your statement or are you sticking with it? Because of course we know it isn't true. You and Miss Rundell were not in the Golden Paradise on Saturday evening. You must have known we were bound to find that out. But no doubt you had your reasons for saying what you did, perhaps pressure from Miss Rundell being one of them. If you'd like to change your statement now, however, we'd be interested to hear the truth.'

'The truth!' Ivor said bitterly. 'When are people like you interested in the truth? If you saw it staring you in the face, you wouldn't believe in it. You've got your own set of ideas of how people behave. You go by the rule book. What's the point of talking to you?'

'The only lie I'm sure you told me,' Patrick said, 'is that you and Miss Rundell were at the Golden Paradise on Saturday evening.'

'Who says?'

'The proprietor. A very respectable Chinese, who knows you both by sight and says you were in his restaurant the Saturday before, but not the night before last.'

'And I thought they couldn't tell one white from another!' Ivor gave a mocking laugh. 'I stick to it, we were there, and this proprietor, whatever his name is, happened not to be looking in our direction at the time.'

'Yet you weren't surprised to see us here this morning,' Patrick said, 'and you walked in just now prepared to do battle.'

'I'm always prepared to do battle with you lot,' Ivor answered. 'Whether it's for having one's driving licence endorsed for something one never did, or murdering one's boss, one's a fool if one admits anything. I've a lawyer friend who told me that. If you're ever in trouble with the police, he said, never say anything. It can always be used against you. But if you say nothing it can't do you any harm. So I'm not saying anything and so you might as well leave.'

'As of now,' Patrick said, 'you aren't in trouble. But false statements, told from whatever motive, only create unnecessary difficulties for us. We have to get them sorted out. And I'd better tell you that your landlady knows you weren't out. She heard your gramophone going all the evening.'

'Ah.' A little to Patrick's surprise, there was a sound of relief in Ivor's voice. He hitched himself on to a stool, picked up an empty test-tube and started fiddling with it. 'You've jumped to the conclusion Isobel spent the evening with me. Well, what if she did? It's true, of course, but we didn't want her father to know it. He's the possessive type. Doesn't want the girl to call her soul her own. No doubt something to do with his wife walking out on him. To himself I expect he explains it as not wanting the child to go the same way as her mother, but the truth is it's a plain case of incestuous jealousy. And if he knew that Isobel had spent the evening with me, he'd leap to the worst possible conclusions. Whereas all we did was drink cider – she's still at the cider age – and sit and listen to records.'

'Where did you eat?'

'*Eat?*' Ivor said, looking startled, as if to eat were the limit of human eccentricity.

'You didn't eat at the Golden Paradise,' Patrick said patiently. 'But at Miss Rundell's age food is still a major consideration. Most seventeen-year-olds that I've ever encountered barely manage to survive from one meal to the next without feeling they're in danger of starvation. I can't see her being satisfied for a whole evening with cider and records.'

'No, of course not,' Ivor agreed with one of his rare smiles. 'Actually we picked up some fish and chips before we went up to my room.'

'Where did you get the fish and chips?'

'At Bruno's Fish Bar.'

'Did you go in for them by yourself, or did you go in together?'

Ivor's smile disappeared. He looked truculent again. 'By myself. Look, what the hell are you getting at? You come in saying I didn't tell you the truth about Saturday evening. All right, I didn't. I've admitted it, haven't I? And I've told you why I didn't. It was to help stop the kid getting into trouble with her bloody father. Then you start asking me where I bought our fish and chips. What d'you mean to make out of that? Does it matter if I say we ate stuffed peacock, so long as we were together? That's all you really want to know, isn't it? Do we alibi each other?'

'Well, I do remember Miss Rundell saying that she doesn't eat potatoes,' Patrick said mildly, 'but perhaps when the delights of fish and chips are offered, she can't resist them.'

The young man scowled at him from under his bushy eyebrows. Then all of a sudden he grinned and the grin developed into a laugh. His face became surprisingly attractive.

'I'm sorry, I've been getting you all wrong,' he said. 'You aren't a bad sort of bloke really. Of course you've been trying to trip me up, but that's just doing your job, isn't it? And characters like me who lie quite happily when it happens to suit them must get badly under your skin. No hard feelings. But Isobel and I did have fish and chips and cider and we did listen to records. Go and ask Bruno. He probably remembers me coming in. We generally have a word about the weather and so on. But I don't understand why you think it's important to check up on us. Do you seriously think either Isobel or I could have killed Dr Gair?'

'I take all discrepancies fairly seriously,' Patrick answered. 'I knew you'd lied about going to the Golden Paradise. The question was why, and where you'd really been.'

'Well, now you know.'

'Yes, I know. Or I know what you've told me.'

Patrick and Farley went to the door.

A moment after they had passed through it and closed it behind them, Patrick reopened it and looked in. Ivor had the telephone to his ear. But without speaking into it, he thoughtfully replaced it on its stand.

'Of course, she wouldn't be at home,' Patrick said from the doorway. 'She's a schoolgirl, isn't she? She'll be at school at this hour of the day. You'll have to wait till some time in the afternoon to let her know what you've told us.'

Ivor whirled round, rage blazing in his blue eyes.

Patrick withdrew again and he and Farley walked away down the corridor.

'Were you serious about the girl not eating chips?' Farley asked. 'Do you think he was lying again?'

Patrick laughed. 'I haven't an idea. But he said himself he lied quite happily when it suited him. We'll have to talk to the girl herself. But I don't want to haul her out of the school to do it. And I'd like to do it when her father isn't there, but if he insists on sitting in on it, there's not much we can do about it.'

'Then you think she's mixed up in the thing somehow?'

'Any of them could be, as I see things at present.' Patrick did not want to talk to anyone yet, even Farley, about the pattern that had begun to form in his mind.

As they went down the stairs they found that the staff

meeting had broken up. A door into what looked like a board-room was open and people were standing about in groups outside it. A number of them were talking eagerly, but they all grew silent when the two detectives appeared. Hugh Rundell gave them only a brief glance, then hurried off to his room. Patrick followed him.

'Mr Rundell.'

Hugh stopped and turned round. He was in a neat dark suit and was wearing a black tie. His face was pasty and it had a mulish look on it, as if he had decided that it was none of his business to co-operate with the police.

'Mr Rundell, I'd like another talk with your daughter today,' Patrick said, 'but I take it she's at school at the moment. Can you tell me when I'll be able to see her?'

'I can't see why you should want to see her at all,' Hugh said. His voice was as level as usual, but there was a gleam of angry curiosity in his eyes. 'She's only seventeen, she's a child, and she can't tell you anything that all the rest of us can't. Have you got to hound her?'

'I only want to straighten out one or two things,' Patrick said.

'Such as?'

'Nothing very important.'

'Well, she'll be home around four o'clock,' Hugh said. 'But I'll be there too this time. I'm not going to have her bullied or frightened for no reason except that you don't know who else to go to work on. I don't know what she told you yesterday to make you suspicious of her, but whatever it was, you can take it from me it was just fantasy. Her imagination is a little too vivid for her own good. She gets carried away by it. But any fool can see through her. There's nothing to be gained by making an issue of it.'

'We aren't suspicious of her,' Patrick said. 'It's just a case of tidying up some loose ends.'

'Well, she'll be at home round about four o'clock,' Hugh repeated.

'Thank you,' Patrick said. 'Then I'll be there.'

He turned away and Hugh Rundell went on into his room,

shutting the door behind him with sudden violence.

Outside the entrance to the building, standing on the gravel drive, Farley observed, 'That's a frightened man. More frightened than he was yesterday. What's happened to him since then?'

'Perhaps he knows his daughter didn't go out to dinner and the cinema with Haydon,' Patrick answered, 'and he's afraid of finding out what they really did. Now I'm going over to see Mrs Bayne. And you might go back into town and check up at Bruno's about those fish and chips. Take the car. I'll get back on the bus presently.' He paused. 'Check up if Haydon bought one portion or two, if Bruno remembers.'

Farley gave him a thoughtful look, but made no comment. He walked off towards the car while Patrick went towards the opening into the courtyard between the Director's and the Deputy Director's houses.

Chapter 12

He found it a seething mass of reporters and photographers. Valerie Bayne was in her doorway, trying to keep them at bay. She was looking rather scared, but was doing her best to answer questions coherently, as if she had decided that that was the easiest way to persuade the mob to leave her alone.

As soon as they saw Patrick, they turned on him, surging about him, throwing questions and clicking shutters at him. He gave them a few minutes, telling them that the dead man in the cupboard had been identified by his son as Dr José Barragan, who had been missing for over a year, but that nothing was known at present of how he had got into the cupboard. Yes, Patrick said, the mummification of the body was a very extraordinary feature of the case, but was not unique. And he had no statement to make on the death of Dr Gair. The inquests on both men would be held on Thursday. After he had said that he shouldered his way to the door and asked Valerie if he could come in.

She looked relieved to have him there. As soon as he was in the room, she shut the door on the crowd outside.

'Edmund told me to tell them anything they wanted to know,' she said. 'He said it would be the quickest way of getting rid of them. How d'you think they found out what's happened? Who told them?'

'Probably someone at the Martindale has a contact with the local Press,' Patrick said, 'and several of them would have contacts with the nationals. That cupboard's bizarre enough to bring them all.'

'Yes.' She gave Patrick one of her long, searching stares. 'Did you come to see me for any special reason?'

He had had a distinctly special reason for coming. He

wanted to find out if she had the same effect upon him this morning as she had had the day before. But that was by the way.

'I was on the spot, and I thought you might like to know they remember you at the Bellringers',' he said.

She nodded gravely. 'I thought they would. Would you like some coffee?'

'I should very much.'

'Then sit down. It won't take me long.'

She disappeared into the kitchen.

Patrick sat down on the sofa and picked up a newspaper that was lying on it. It was the local *Herald* and a report of the murder, though a brief one, was on the front page. He was reading it when Valerie returned with two cups on a tray.

'You may like to know,' she said, 'that my brother knows all about my night out. If you happen to want to mention it to him, there's no reason why you shouldn't.'

He smiled. 'Did you decide to tell him, or how did he find out?'

'I told him when I discovered he knew I hadn't been at the Botanical Society meeting. One of the Martindale people told him I hadn't been there. So then he got it into his head I might have been the person Dr Gair was expecting to dinner, and I thought I'd better put him right.'

'I didn't really understand why you minded his knowing what you'd been doing,' Patrick said.

'Nor do I now that he and I have talked about it. I've a feeling he understands it better than I do. He's a remarkably understanding person, you know. He seems so absent-minded, but he knows a lot about people. And he told me he'd noticed for some time I was getting restless, and thought that sooner or later I'd go away. He urged me to go back to university and get some post-graduate training and then try for some good sort of job. I thought on Saturday evening, when I went off alone, that if I told him that was the sort of thing I had in mind, he'd be against it. I've tried to talk about it once or twice before and he's always taken it as a way of saying that I wasn't happy with him. And it would be horribly ungrateful to let him think that, because coming to live with him was a life-saver for me when my husband was killed.' She paused. She gave him a slightly puzzled look, as if she wondered why she talked to him so readily. 'But this isn't the sort of thing you want to talk about,' she said.

'What did you do when you were at the university?' he asked.

'History. To boast a bit, I actually got a First, and I was all set to start on research when I got married instead. My husband was a mining engineer and we went to live in Newcastle, and unless I'd done a teacher's training course and settled for teaching, which didn't attract me, I couldn't have got much of a job. And anyway, I didn't want one at the time. I thought we were going to have children. And after I came here I did a number of odd voluntary jobs to while the time away, but I was horribly unreliable about them and always managed to think up some good reason for dropping them. But I think if I get back into my own line now, I'll stick to it.'

He nearly told her that if he had gone to a university, he too would have taken history. But his interest in it was a very private matter, about which he was not in the habit of confiding in people.

'If you do that, I suppose you'll be going away,' he said.

'Yes, back to London.'

It was the sharpness of the disappointment that he felt that made him finish his coffee quickly and stand up. He had no business to be feeling disappointment, or anything else in particular, in connection with this woman. But the truth was, as he had suddenly realized, she had a lovely profile which it was a deep pleasure to contemplate, and there was a grace about her too which acted very strongly upon him. And besides that, he sensed that she responded to him more than she herself was aware, and that stirred up thoughts in him that were not appropriate to the time and place. She was merely a person involved in a case of which he happened to be in charge. Or, as you might put it, a character in a drama which he had the job of directing. Not a drama in which he himself had a part. He was outside it and it was important that he should stay there.

When he left he walked to the bottom of the drive, then caught the next bus into Keyfield. He had a lunch of beer and sausage rolls in the Green Man, a pub near the police station, then went on to it, went to his office and settled down to do some telephoning.

His first call was to an Inspector Luttrell at Scotland Yard who had been in charge of the Barragan disappearance. What was the name of the restaurant, Patrick wanted to know, to which Dr Barragan had presumably been going when he vanished?

It was Neville's, he was told, in Uphall Street. That confirmed what young Dr Barragan had told him.

Had any investigation been made of the people who had dined at Neville's that evening, Patrick asked next.

No, that had not been thought necessary, since Dr Barragan had never reached the place.

Had any investigation been made of anyone else who had made a reservation for that evening and not reached the place?

No, said a slightly disconcerted voice, that had not been thought necessary either. Was there any specific reason for that particular inquiry?

Just a tenuous idea at the back of his mind, Patrick replied, thanking the speaker and putting the telephone down.

His next call was to Neville's Restaurant. Identifying himself, he asked if they kept records of their table reservations for as long as a year ago. Unfortunately, no, he was told.

So that was a dead end. Patrick could not prove that Charles Gair had had a reservation at Neville's on the evening of Dr Barragan's disappearance and, like the Mexican, had failed to arrive. All the same, Patrick decided, there was a distinct probability that it had been in the entrance of the restaurant, or perhaps in the bar, that the two men had encountered one another that evening. Having met, of course, at least once before.

Patrick picked up the telephone for a third time.

Could Mrs Bayne tell him, he asked, if Dr Gair had been in the habit of dining at Neville's in Uphall Street?

He could, of course, have asked them this at Neville's, but

that would not have given him an opportunity to listen to Valerie's voice.

'Why, yes,' she replied, and sounded pleased to be able to answer one of his questions helpfully. 'He took my brother and me to dinner there once, and I remember they seemed to know him quite well. He liked that. It makes one feel so grand, doesn't it, being recognized in restaurants? It's a place that goes in for traditional English cooking and a Victorian sort of luxury. Very good, in its way, and very expensive.'

'I see. Thanks.' Patrick hesitated. He wanted, just for the sake of listening to her, to go on talking, but he could not think of a single thing to say. He rang off abruptly.

At four o'clock, with Sergeant Farley, who had reported that Bruno thought he remembered that Ivor Haydon had bought only one portion of fish and chips on Saturday evening, Patrick arrived at the Rundells' house.

It was in a crescent of medium-sized detached houses, built about ten years before. They had been carefully designed not to look exactly alike, although their basic plans were probably identical. Some were of red brick, some were of white rough-cast, some had wood panels on their façades. They all looked out over a semi-circle of lawn, dotted with clumps of lilacs and azaleas. Most of them had names as well as numbers.

The Rundells' house, which was of red brick, had the best-kept garden in the crescent. There was not a weed to be seen in the front lawn. The low privet hedge which enclosed it might have been trimmed with the aid of a spirit level. A round bed in the middle of the lawn was filled with stiff pink hyacinths.

When Patrick rang the bell, the door was opened by Hugh. His greeting was cool, but not as unfriendly as Patrick had expected. Hugh took the two detectives into a room that over-looked the back garden, which was as impeccably, unimaginatively neat as the front. The room, by contrast, looked un-cared-for. It was furnished with a three-piece suite covered in faded cretonne and some reproduction furniture which had never been good and was not standing up well to the test of time. The wall-to-wall carpeting was spotty and looked dusty around the edges. Patrick deduced that Rundell paid a not very efficient woman to clean the house for him, but looked after the garden himself.

'My daughter hasn't come back yet,' Hugh said, 'but she'll be in any minute now. She won't be expecting you.' After a moment, he added, 'I wish I understood why you want to see her.'

They had all sat down, Patrick and the sergeant side by side on the sofa, of which the sergeant took up a good deal more than his fair share. Hugh faced them from the far side of the fireplace.

'I suppose there's no reason why I shouldn't tell you,' Patrick said. He had begun to think, since Rundell was going to be present at the interview, that it might be useful to let him know what it was about. 'It's simply that her account of how she and Dr Haydon spent Saturday evening happens to be untrue. They didn't dine at the Golden Paradise. And that's probably of no importance to anyone but themselves. All the same, I'd like to know what they actually did.'

'They didn't . . .' Hugh began. A tight frown creased his forehead. 'But they said, they both said . . .' He paused again.

'I know,' Patrick said. 'But the proprietor of the place knows them and remembers quite well that they were there the Saturday before last, but not the day before yesterday.'

'Have you spoken to Haydon about this?' Hugh asked.

'I have, as a matter of fact.'

'And what did he say about where they'd been?'

'Mr Rundell, it's what your daughter has to say about where they were that I'm interested in now,' Patrick answered. 'Perhaps she won't tell me the same as Dr Haydon.'

Hugh gave a hard little laugh. 'You don't think I'd coach her, do you? If she's been lying to me, as she's got rather a habit of doing, she can get herself out of the mess by herself. I've been thinking about that since you spoke to me this morning. I was scared for her at first, and thought I might cover up whatever she's been up to. But she's got to learn to take responsibility for her own actions sometime. If she was with Haydon, if she was in his room with him, well, she can tell you that. She's got to learn that there are situations where lying doesn't help. At present she believes there's nothing she can say that won't be believed if it's said with a sort of wide-eyed innocence. Innocence!' There was a sudden blaze of desperation in his eyes. 'Her mother has it, that same innocent – yes, it is a kind of innocence! – that same belief that she can get away with anything. And no real feelings to go with it, nothing deep or real ...' He caught his breath. 'I'm sorry, I didn't mean to talk about my private affairs. Here's Isobel.'

He hurried out of the room at the sound of the front door opening and closing.

Patrick could hear what Hugh said to his daughter in the hall. He did not coach her. He only told her that Superintendent Dunn was here and wanted a word with her. She came quickly to the sitting-room and glanced in, a very different-looking girl from the one whom Patrick and Farley had seen on Sunday morning. She was in a school uniform, a purple and white checked gingham dress with a purple blazer over it. She had a purple beret on the back of her head. A satchel of books was slung over one shoulder. The effect was to make her appear to have shed at least two years since the day before. Seeing the two men, her cheeks went pink, as if they had caught her out indecently dressed, and muttering something about being only a minute, she vanished from the room.

They heard her racing up the stairs and then her quick footsteps going to and fro in the room above their heads. After about five minutes she reappeared, dressed in jeans, curious-looking wooden clogs and a shirt of blazing colours. Perching on the arm of a chair, she put on a smile of deliberate provocation.

'Well now, what can I do for you?' she asked with slightly laboured gaiety.

'It concerns Saturday evening,' Patrick said. 'In your statement to us yesterday you said that you and Dr Haydon had dinner at the Golden Paradise.'

Hugh did not let him get any further. Both his fists came up, as if he would have liked to strike his daughter.

'And that was another of your lies!' he said in a voice that was almost a whisper. There was something eerie, Patrick thought, about the way that Hugh Rundell never raised his voice, however violent his emotions might be. If he ever did entirely lose control of himself, it might be interesting to see what happened to him. 'At your age – a schoolgirl – a mere child! Going to Haydon's room with him, spending the evening there with him – it's obscene, it's foul!'

So, after all, he had coached her, if that had been his intention.

But the effect of his coaching could not have been as he had foreseen it.

Her golden-brown eyes sparkling with intense rage, Isobel shouted at him, 'I'm seventeen, I'm not a child! And it's you who's lying. I wasn't with Ivor!'

'You're a stupid, ignorant, heartless child,' he whispered back at her. 'I'll be glad when I've seen the last of you, as I have of your mother.' Then he seemed to take in what she had said. 'You *weren't* with Haydon?'

'No, I wasn't!' she nearly shrieked. 'I don't give a damn for Ivor. He's a conceited bore. When I sleep with a man, it's going to be someone quite different. Because that's what you're saying, isn't it? You're saying I've been sleeping with Ivor.'

Hugh winced, as if he could not stand the bald statement from her.

'I didn't say ... I only asked ...' he floundered. His eyes were confused. There were small patches of red on his pale cheeks. 'Haydon himself said you spent the evening with him at the Golden Paradise, but you weren't at the Golden Paradise, so naturally – '

'So *naturally* you hadn't the sense to realize I *asked* him to say we were at the Golden Paradise,' she cried mockingly. 'He came here yesterday morning to find out why I'd put him off the evening before, and I asked him to say I'd been with him, and he said all right, he didn't mind. That was when you telephoned to tell me about Charles and I thought it might save me getting into some trouble. But I won't have you saying Ivor's my lover, I *won't* have it!'

'Trouble?' Hugh said. 'What other trouble have you been getting into?'

'Nothing,' she said quickly. 'Nothing at all. I just thought if we said we'd been together, no one could ask us any questions. I thought it would save us *both* trouble.'

Hugh advanced a step towards her. 'What other trouble have you been getting into? And no more lies about it.'

She shot a wild look at Patrick, as if help might come from him. Her eyes suddenly swam with tears.

'You're so blind,' she told her father. 'A thing can be right under your nose and you don't see it. Don't you know that Charles was terribly in love with me? Everyone else knew. I bet everyone but you at the Martindale knew all about it. Don't you understand even now I was the woman he was expecting on Saturday evening? That's why I got my new dress and had my hair done and got you to let me have the car. I'd never actually had dinner with Charles before. I'd never been to his house alone before. And then – and then – '

Her voice shook and she began to sob uncontrollably. Hugh stood staring at her, looking dazed, as if she had changed into some sort of unrecognizable monster in front of his eyes.

'He stood me up,' she went on. 'I *thought* he stood me up. I went to the door and I knocked and I knocked and he didn't come. And I thought he'd forgotten all about me. I thought he hadn't meant it seriously when he asked me to dine with him. I thought he must have been teasing me, because I was only seventeen. So I went away and I didn't go home, because I didn't want you asking me what had gone wrong with my evening. I went to the Singing Kettle and I had poached eggs and some cream buns – ' She swung round on Patrick again. 'You can check that up, if you want to, and they'll remember me all right, because I sat there crying most of the time. I simply couldn't stop myself. And I hardly slept at all all night and when I started crying next morning it was all because of what Charles had done to me, it had nothing to do with Mummy's letter. I've quite grown out of doing that ever again. And then – then I heard about Charles being dead and I realized he hadn't meant to stand me up at all and that I'd misunderstood everything. But I didn't want anyone to know I was the woman he'd been expecting, so I got Ivor to give me an alibi, although of course I don't really care what people say about me. But just to be on the safe side, I thought, it'd be a sensible thing to do. And Ivor didn't mind. He'll always do anything I ask him.'

Hugh slowly let out a breath that he had been holding.

'I'm almost glad Charles is dead,' he muttered, 'or I'm not sure what I might do. And I seem to have underrated Haydon. He's certainly generous.' He laid a hand on the girl's shoulder. It was an uneasy gesture, but there was affection in it. 'It would help so much, though, if you trusted me a little more.' He looked at Patrick. 'Does that tell you everything you want to know?'

'I think so.' Patrick stood up. 'Oh – there's just one thing, Miss Rundell. When you were knocking at Dr Gair's door, did you see anything or hear anything that made you think there was anyone inside?'

She mopped her eyes and gave her nose a blow.

'I heard the dogs, that's all, as if he'd shut them up in the house and gone out. That's why I thought he'd just forgotten me.'

'There wasn't any car except your own in the drive?'

'No, nothing.'

'Then that's all, I think,' Patrick said. 'Thank you.'

Hugh Rundell showed him and the sergeant out.

In his car on the way back to the police station, Farley observed, 'Of course, now Haydon hasn't got an alibi any more.'

'No,' Patrick agreed.

'And he's got a motive, hasn't he?'

'If he knew about the girl's appointment with Gair.'

'She said he didn't until she herself told him next day. But she also said everyone at the Martindale knew about the affair.'

'They probably did too.'

'So Haydon might easily have guessed where she was going

when she cancelled her evening with him. And doesn't it seem more likely Haydon'd lie to give himself an alibi than to cover up his girl-friend's affair with someone else?'

'On the face of it, yes.'

'But you don't think so?'

Patrick took a moment to answer. 'I was really thinking about something else. Something that's been on my mind since last night. But I'm not sure, actually, how the mind of a man like Haydon works. I'm not sure he wouldn't give the girl an alibi out of sheer pleasure at making things a bit more difficult for us. And out of a sort of good nature towards the girl herself. I don't believe she's extremely important to him, but I think he's quite fond of her.'

'Yes, maybe. He did seem kind of relieved when we jumped to the conclusion his not being at the Golden Paradise with the girl meant they'd been up in his room.'

'That's true, he did.'

Farley stopped the car at some traffic-lights. He glanced sideways at Patrick's thoughtful profile.

'This thing that's been on your mind,' Farley said, 'would it have something to do with that Mexican and his son, who's arrived so mighty conveniently on the spot just now?'

'It's mostly about the cupboard,' Patrick said. 'I've been thinking, if you had a cupboard in your house that did what that one does to dead bodies, how would you ever find it out unless you'd had at least one other body in there before? But what would make you stuff a dead body in a cupboard at all if you didn't know what the cupboard would do?'

The car moved on again.

'Well, if you were taken by surprise, say, and had to get it out of sight in a hurry,' Farley suggested.

'Yes,' Patrick agreed, 'that's just what I thought. And I've been making up a kind of story in my head, Jim. Suppose you were expecting guests for drinks – a visiting American scientist and some people you'd asked to meet him. And just a little while before they're due, you have a quarrel with your wife. You've always gone in for having public mock-quarrels with her, but this one is private and it's serious. And you kill her.

110

Perhaps you meant to, perhaps it was an accident, but there she is on your hands, dead. So the only thing you can think of doing is bundling her out of sight into the cupboard in your cellar. You think when it's dark you'll be able to get rid of the corpse somewhere else. And you receive your guests and your behaviour's odd enough, as it well might be, for everyone to notice it. But they think it's because, as you tell them, your wife's just left you. Then you do a stupid thing. You insist on driving your distinguished visitor to the station yourself. You do it to show how carefree you are, but the truth is, you aren't fit to drive. And you smash the car into a tree and you wake up in hospital. And you realize that even if the body hasn't been found yet, by the time they let you out it's going to be far gone in decay and smelling to high heaven. It isn't as if the house would be left empty while you're away. You've a daily woman who goes in to clean in the mornings, and she'd soon notice something. And just possibly you're a man who might face being hanged – I don't know about that, but you're a fairly wild sort of character with a love of drama, so perhaps you could face that. But you can't face the long years in prison. No chance to do your scientific work, to garden, to paint, to play the piano. That you really can't face. So one day you swallow a bottle of barbiturates. But they pull you round. And then you begin to get puzzled. Nobody's saying anything to you about a body in a cupboard. There's total silence on the subject. So you do nothing more about things till they send you home, and then, of course, you find out what's actually happened. You've got a mummy on your hands.'

'But you've still got to get rid of that, haven't you, to make room for the Mexican?' Farley said. 'How do you go about that?'

'You start building a rockery, don't you?' Patrick replied. 'We've been told Gair started on the rockery and seemed to cheer up wonderfully quite soon after his wife left him. Well, one night near the beginning of the operation, your dead wife goes into the foundations and you heap stones on top of her. And you plant aubretia and gold dust and dwarf azaleas and whatnot, and there you are. You've every reason to cheer up wonderfully. You've got away with murder.'

The car had stopped in front of the police station. The two men got out of it and went in at the entrance. Farley was looking at Patrick with a certain awe.

'Of course, there may be some fatal flaw in all this,' Patrick said, 'but I know the next thing I mean to do is get permission to take that rockery to pieces.'

Chapter 13

The next morning Valerie took the car and went into Keyfield to do some shopping. It was a cool, windy morning with clouds scurrying across the sky and sudden shafts of sunshine gleaming down between them. The countryside was chequered with a patchwork of brightness and shade. Edmund had gone over to the Station at the usual time, but had said that he would not be home for lunch. He was expecting Sir Timothy Speight and thought that he would probably have to take him out to lunch.

As she drove into Keyfield Valerie was wondering what Edmund would do if she carried out her half-formed plan of going back to study. Would he stay on in the house on the estate or perhaps find himself a small flat in the town? A flat in which his clothes and books and papers and gramophone records could spread unchecked in every direction, each object settling into a place uniquely its own and as easy for him to find as in the moderate order that she had imposed upon him and which perhaps he had never found really congenial. A protesting daily help would be taught to dust only round the very edges of things, but would soon come to love Edmund and to tolerate his eccentricities with an amused sort of veneration. Valerie had seen that happen before. Life might work out very well for him.

She found this a slightly chilling thought. It had never occurred to her before to strip herself of the comfort of being needed. Then suddenly she wished that she could pack up and leave Keyfield that very day. The tension of the week-end behind her and the thought of its going on and on for days and days seemed all at once unbearable. She wanted to flee from it all as if she herself were at the heart of the mystery and somehow threatened, entangled in the cobweb strands of suspicion that were beginning to form delicately and distortingly from face to face around her, just as the thick, dusty cobwebs in Charles Gair's cupboard had draped themselves concealingly over nose and jaw and cheekbones of the dead man inside.

For an instant a vision of that incredible sight, as Hugh had revealed it to her and Edmund in the cellar, completely filled her imagination. She felt the same shock and horror as she had felt then. Her head swam. She was glad to turn the car into a parking space most fortunately close to the supermarket in the High Street, which was her destination, pick her two large shopping baskets off the seat beside her and go into the store.

For the next ten minutes she drifted with a trolley up and down the lanes of the supermarket, collecting washing powder, soap, polish, butter, eggs, bacon, cheese, bread, rice, curry powder, until all of a sudden, making her way between two tall columns of tinned soups, she came face to face with Isobel Rundell.

Isobel was not alone. Just behind her stood Alberti Barragan, who was pushing a trolley full of groceries, looking somehow surprised at himself for having got involved in this woman's work. Isobel was wearing a droopy ankle-length cotton dress in a pattern of black and purple cartwheels and had several long strings of beads round her neck. Her shining hair was spread out round her shoulders.

'Oh, hallo, Val,' she said, looking quite pleased at the meeting. She had, after all, a trophy to show off. 'This is Alberti. He came to see us yesterday because of my father finding his father. And I'm looking after him, because of course he's a complete stranger here and needs someone to take care of him. Don't you, Alberti?'

The young Mexican gave a rather bewildered smile and nodded and gave Valerie a grave little bow.

'Dr Barragan and I have met,' Valerie said. 'Why aren't you at school this morning, Isobel?'

'Because I've left!' The girl did an excited little dance-step between the tins of soup. 'I've at last persuaded Daddy there really wasn't any point in my going on. I was just wasting my time there when I could so easily have been doing something

114

much more interesting and educational. And after all, I've got my A levels, so I can go to university later if I want to. Val, Alberti and I were just going across to the Singing Kettle to have a cup of coffee. Won't you come with us?'

For Isobel it was a generous invitation. She usually liked to have a man to herself. But perhaps having just that day shaken off the shackles of childhood, she was in an expansive mood. Valerie said that she would be delighted to join them if she could just finish her shopping first and they separated down different tunnels of goods to meet again about ten minutes later at one of the small round tables in the Singing Kettle.

There was a party of wives from the Martindale, Myrtle Fullerton, Ruth Isaacs and Wendy Conners, sitting at another table in the café. Ruth was a small, compact, handsome woman of about Valerie's own age, who had a family of five, yet who managed to have enough spare time to be secretary of the Keyfield Botanical Society and to sit on various other committees. Wendy was a thin, vague woman of forty, whose husband was a cytologist, working on polyploidy in blackberries. The three women looked surprised when Valerie only waved to them and did not join them, but went instead to sit with Isobel and Alberti Barragan at their table in the window. They both had cups of coffee and Isobel was eating a large wedge of squashy-looking cake, in her view evidently not so dangerous to her figure as potatoes.

'I'm so happy!' she exclaimed as Valerie sat down at the table and ordered coffee. 'Oh no, I don't mean that, of course not, not *happy*! Alberti, I didn't mean that. Because it's all so terribly tragic for you, I do understand that, and I couldn't feel more sympathetic.' Isobel put a hand on his wrist. 'I understand it because of course I've suffered a loss myself. And not the first in my life. It's a terrible thing, losing a person who's dear to you.'

Alberti Barragan smiled.

'Please be happy – Isobel.' He brought the christian name out with an effort, as if it were an idiom he was trying to master in this difficult foreign language. 'It becomes you.'

'It becomes me – doesn't that sound lovely, Val?' Isobel said delightedly. She kept hold of the young man's wrist with one hand while forking up cake with the other. 'I love the way he talks. It all sounds specially serious and meaningful somehow. But it's a terrible situation for him, being under suspicion and everything.'

'Under suspicion?' Valerie asked. She looked into Alberti Barragan's dark eyes. 'She can't mean that, surely.'

'Only, I think, in the sense that we are all under suspicion,' he answered. 'I told you yesterday, I have no alibi for Saturday night. And I have a motive. As I have told the police myself, if I had known the truth about my father's murder, I would not have hesitated to kill Dr Gair with my own hands.'

'Darling, you should never have said a thing like that!' Isobel said. 'I mean, our police are wonderful and everything, but you don't want to trust them too far. That could be just the sort of thing they'll use against you. And as a matter of fact, Charles wasn't as bad as all that. As a matter of fact, I was very fond of him. As a matter of fact, I was . . .' She stopped abruptly. Bright colour flooded her cheeks. 'Oh well,' she went on a little uncertainly, 'there's no reason I shouldn't tell you, because I expect it's all over the Martindale by now, but I was the woman Charles was expecting to dinner.' Having brought it out, she drew herself up, looking sad, dignified and as much like a real woman as she could. Valerie wondered if Isobel ever altogether stopped acting. 'That chicken casserole he was cooking, and which I know would have been fabulous, was meant for me. And I've never felt as terrible as I did that night when I thought he'd fogotten me. That's partly what I meant when I said I knew what it's like to lose a person who's dear to you. Charles and my mother – I've lost them both.'

Valerie was suddenly aware that the café was unusually quiet except for the sound of Isobel's clear voice. The three Martindale wives were all silent and without exactly looking towards their table, had their attention obviously focused upon it.

To check any more of Isobel's revelations, Valerie said,

'Now that you've left school, Isobel, have you decided what you're going to do?'

'My father and I talked about that last night,' Isobel answered. 'We think it would be a good idea if I went as an *au pair* girl for a year to Switzerland or somewhere. Then I'd be old enough to go to university, though I'm not at all sure that I want to do that. Unless perhaps I decided to be a doctor. I'd like to be a doctor and help people. Alberti, what do you think about that?'

Alberti looked startled and mildly horrified, but answered gently, 'You have plenty of time to make up your mind.'

'But time passes so quickly,' Isobel said with a deep sigh. 'The older one gets, the faster it goes. Only last week you and I had never met, and yet now I seem to have known you for years. And that terrible discovery about Charles and your father hadn't happened, and yet now that seems an eternity ago.'

'It does,' Valerie agreed.

'And now Alberti and I had better be going,' Isobel said, standing up. 'I promised my father I'd get lunch for him and Alberti's coming back to have it with us. Well, good-bye, Val. It was nice seeing you.'

Making sure that Alberti had gathered up all her shopping-bags and parcels, Isobel led the way out of the café.

As soon as they had gone Myrtle, Ruth and Wendy descended on Valerie, who had not quite finished her coffee. They planted themselves on the other chairs at the table.

'Val, we couldn't help hearing,' Myrtle said. 'That girl always talks at the top of her voice. But she did say, didn't she, that she was the person Charles was expecting to dinner on Saturday?'

'She said so, yes,' Valerie said.

'Well, isn't that just what I told you yesterday?' Myrtle said with satisfaction. 'I told you I was a good guesser. You'd be surprised how often I'm right about people. Oswald sometimes says I've a sort of sixth sense. I told you I saw them in here together and knew at once there was something in it. And I must say, even for Charles, I think it was going a bit far, going to work on a child like that. Unless, of course, it was the other way round and Charles just took the line of least resistance. Isobel's shockingly over-sexed. You only had to watch her with that young man this morning. She probably did her best to seduce Charles. It's the result of losing her mother when she did, you know. She had a most unfortunate adolescence. One ought to be sorry for her.'

'I *am* very sorry for her,' Wendy Conners said. 'With this awful thing happening today about her father. Perhaps she doesn't know about it yet, but it's really grim, isn't it?'

'Something awful happened about Hugh today?' Valerie said.

'I don't believe it myself,' Ruth Isaacs said. 'Not of Hugh. If it was Charles now, I might believe it, but it can't be true of Hugh.'

'I don't understand,' Valerie said. 'What happened?'

'The books, my dear,' Myrtle explained. 'You haven't heard? The police have taken charge of the books of the Station and are having them examined by accountants. That's why Speight's here today. I suppose he had to be told what they were going to do. And of course, if there's anything wrong with them, that gives Hugh a motive for doing away with Charles, because you know if there'd been the slightest irregularity, Charles would have had Hugh out on his ear in a twinkling. Those two detested one another. If Charles could have found the slightest excuse for getting rid of Hugh, he wouldn't have hesitated.'

'But d'you mean there's some evidence of irregularity, as you call it?' Valerie asked.

'No, there isn't,' Ruth Isaacs said. 'It's obviously just a routine check, something the police have got to do as a matter of course in a case like this. And they won't find anything. Hugh's as scrupulous as they come. If it had been Charles who was supposed to have fiddled the books, I might believe in it, except that he'd have been too cunning to leave any evidence against himself around, but I simply don't believe it of Hugh. And I'm not saying that because he's a particularly

118

close friend of mine. He isn't. He's too stiff and prickly for my liking. But I'm utterly convinced he's honesty itself.'

'And so am I,' Valerie said. 'Of course it's only a routine check.'

'What I think,' Wendy Conners said, 'is that perhaps – I do mean just perhaps, of course – Hugh may have got into far deeper water than any of us know about sending money to that awful wife of his, and so – well, personally I'd hardly blame him, because he's really had such a grim life – but Myrtle's right, Charles would never have seen it that way, and if he'd had the very faintest shadow of an excuse for getting rid of Hugh he'd have snatched at it.'

'But Hugh's never had to send money to Debbie,' Valerie said. 'She never asked for it.'

'So he *says*,' Myrtle said. 'Hugh's very proud, you know. He'd never let on if he was being exploited. He'd hate to be thought weak.'

'But I've seen several of Debbie's letters to him,' Valerie said. 'She never asks for money. And even if she did, he'd never tamper with the funds of the Martindale. Not for that or any other reason. The idea's fantastic.'

'Of course, you never really knew Debbie, did you, Val?' Myrtle said reflectively. 'She left fairly soon after you got here. Hugh was a quite different sort of man in those days. He just lived for her, you know. She could do anything with him. Actually she could do anything with several of the men around here, or anyway, if she couldn't, she thought she could. She had a tremendous amount of vanity, as that sort of woman so often has. She could never believe she wasn't irresistible. She even tried to get her hooks into Oswald once, I remember. Of course, that was just funny. The poor man simply couldn't understand what she was trying to do to him. He kept asking me what I thought was the matter with her. And Edmund too – oh dear, yes, though she really rather preferred married men, because half the fun of it for her was the competition with their wives. That's characteristic too of the type, you know, the need for victory over the other woman. So Edmund wasn't much of a challenge. But Charles – oh dear, yes, Charles!

You know, I've often wondered if his final quarrel with Rhona wasn't over Debbie, and that's why he and Hugh really hated each other so. Of course, that's only a guess, but as I said, I'm a pretty good guesser.'

'None of which has anything to do with Hugh cooking the books,' Ruth said. 'And personally I think this picture of Debbie as the ultimate *femme fatale* is a wild exaggeration. It's a sort of romantic nonsense that's grown with the years since she left.'

'I rather liked her,' Valerie remarked.

'Oh, she was very – well, quite amusing,' Wendy said. 'And she'd be specially nice to you just when she was making a pass at your husband. I remember once with Reg at a party, I found them in the kitchen ... Still, that's ancient history and there wasn't any harm in it. Reg and I laughed a lot about it afterwards. But still, what I think is – if Val's sure Debbie hasn't been asking Hugh for money lately – it might have been all those years ago that she wheedled something out of him he couldn't afford, and he borrowed – that's how he'd have thought of it, just borrowing – some money from the Martindale, and perhaps even replaced it later, because I quite agree he's desperately honest – and then Charles could somehow have happened to find it out just recently, and then, well, there you are.'

'I don't believe any of it,' Ruth said, standing up and collecting her parcels.

'Nor do they,' Valerie said. 'They really believe Debbie was an agent for the Russians, and that Mexican doctor was working for the CIA, and the secret formula's hidden in Hugh's account books, and Charles found out about it and was going to sell the secret to the Chinese, and old Speight's a representative of MI5 who's here trying to hush everything up, because it's obviously he who came down here on Saturday and murdered Charles.'

Ruth laughed. 'Of course. It's all quite simple when you look at it like that, isn't it? Now I must rush home and get the lunch. I've all those hungry mouths to feed.'

She hurried out.

Myrtle and Wendy showed signs of wanting to continue the discussion, but Valerie followed Ruth out and returned to her car.

Chapter 14

On the way back to the Martindale Valerie was not much worried by the thought that the books of the research station were being checked. She supposed that it was inevitable that they should be. But she could imagine that Hugh would be in a state of desperate tension until the job was finished. He was the sort of man to whom a mere investigation of his honesty would seem almost tantamount to an accusation of guilt. So for his sake she hoped that the matter would be settled quickly. She trusted him absolutely. To think of him as a murderer, swept away by some sudden eruption of too much suppressed feeling, was easier than to envisage him as an embezzler, calculating and corrupt.

Driving up to the house, she saw that the police were there once more. There were two cars in the drive and several uniformed men waiting about as if for orders to begin on some operation. As she got out of her car and pulled out her heavy shopping baskets, Patrick Dunn appeared from behind the other men and came towards her.

'Can I help with those?' he suggested.

She gave him one of the baskets to carry. She sensed something new about him this morning, something alert and expectant.

'Are you here for some special reason?' she asked. 'Has anything happened?'

'Just checking a theory,' he answered, following her towards the house. 'But I'd like a few words with you first to make sure I've got certain things straight. Mind if I come in for a few minutes?'

'Of course not.' She unlocked the door. As she went in the two dogs, who had been left shut up in the house while she

122

went into Keyfield, came bounding at her, taking not much notice of her commands to them to be quiet, and barking suspiciously at Patrick. Trying to calm them, she said, 'I'm sorry about them, but they're naturally in a very nervous state. They can't make out what's happened to them.'

'Are you going to keep them?' Patrick asked.

She took her shopping baskets to the kitchen. Returning, she answered, 'I don't suppose so. If I'm going to London, I expect my brother will move into something smaller than this house, perhaps a flat in Keyfield, then he couldn't cope with dogs. I don't know quite what will happen to them. Perhaps if we advertise, we'll find a good home for them. Do sit down.' She sat down herself on the sofa.

But Patrick, instead of sitting down, started moving aimlessly about the room.

'You're still thinking of London, then?' he said.

She heard a kind of remonstrance in his voice, which intrigued her. It could hardly matter to him whether she went or not.

'Fairly definitely. My brother and I have talked it over. He's been urging me to go.' She watched Patrick's restless movements, wondering what he wanted with her that morning, wondering too if the feeling she had that it would turn out to be something of not much importance, because what he actually wanted was merely to talk to her for a little, was as close to the truth as she suddenly sensed.

'I see.' He did not look at her, but picked up a tortoiseshell snuffbox from a table and studied it frowningly.

After a moment, because he seemed to have nothing further to say, Valerie said, 'I've heard that the books of the Martindale are being examined.'

'That's just routine,' he answered. 'It's got to be done, but I'd be surprised if it led to anything.'

'Then this theory you're checking hasn't anything to do with them.'

'Nothing at all. I'll tell you about it. Only first I'd like to ask you something. Can I – ?' He put the snuffbox down and looked at her. 'Can I see that painting of Gair's again?'

It was not at all what she had been expecting and she had a feeling that it was not what he had meant to say, that it was merely a way of marking time.

'I'll bring it,' she said. 'My brother took it down yesterday. He said that he couldn't bear to have it around now that we know what we do about Charles.'

'We still don't know so very much, do we?' Patrick said. 'That's why I'd like to look at the painting again, to see if he seems to be the kind of man I think, or if I'm out of my wits.'

'Just wait a moment.' She went out and returned with the picture.

Setting it down on the sofa, she propped it up against the back. Patrick stood in front of it, staring down at it.

When he had said nothing for some time, Valerie said, 'You seemed to like it when you saw it before.'

'I did,' he answered. 'Now I don't like it at all.'

'Why not?'

'It seems to have changed. When I saw it before I saw it as a sort of vase of poppies. It seemed nice and bright and cheerful.'

'And now?'

'I don't know. It could just as easily be flames coming out of a chimney, couldn't it? Or even – ' He gave a deprecating smile at the workings of his own imagination. 'Even blood gushing from a wound.'

'I've never thought of it as being a picture of anything at all,' Valerie said. 'I've always thought of it as just a rather exciting explosion of colour.'

'You're probably right. And since the thing itself can't have changed in the last three days, the change is obviously in me. But I wouldn't care to have it about the house myself.'

'And what does it do to your theory?'

'Nothing whatever, of course. I knew it wouldn't. I haven't heard of crimes getting solved by art criticism. Not at my level, anyway. Yet I had this feeling of wanting to take another look at the thing. This theory, you see, is that Gair may have been a multiple murderer, may at least have murdered his wife and buried her under the rockery. And it seemed as if the picture might have helped me to look into his mind. An interesting thing, after all, the mind of a man like that. But all it's done is give me a glimpse of my own.'

Valerie's amazed glance was on his face.

'You think Charles murdered *Rhona*?'

'I think it's possible.'

'And buried her under the rockery?'

'Well, didn't he start building the rockery soon after he came out of the hospital?' he asked. 'And has anyone set eyes on Rhona Gair from the day she left Gair till now? And don't you think the cupboard that contained Dr Barragan may very likely have had at least one other body in it before, or how did Gair know it would work? Does that strike you as too fanciful?'

'But not the *rockery*,' Valerie said with a sort of moan in her voice.

He looked puzzled. 'What's special about the rockery?'

'I helped him build it,' she said. 'He hadn't been long out of hospital and he wasn't very strong. He had the stones delivered by a firm of landscape gardeners, but he wouldn't let them make the rockery, he was determined to manage it by himself. So I used to go over and we'd shift the stones between us. And then – then he made something marvellous out of it. It was the bit of the garden that he took most pride in. It hasn't just got commonplace things in it, you know, it's got all sorts of very rare plants that he got sent from all over the world. And he used to give me cuttings and seedlings for ours, only I could never get them to thrive as he did ... You've really got to take it all to pieces?'

'I'm afraid so,' Patrick said. 'That's what the men are here for today. That's what I really came over to tell you. I wanted to warn you that they'd be at work in the garden for some time.'

'Rhona?' Valerie said softly, experimenting with the idea, looking down at the painting on the sofa. 'Rhona murdered too? I've never even thought she could be dead. But if you're wrong ...?'

'I easily may be.'

'I understand you're puzzled about how Charles knew the cupboard would work on Dr Barragan, but he could have found it out by accident, couldn't he?' She looked up suddenly. 'Why did he leave Dr Barragan in the cupboard? Why didn't he bury him in the garden too?'

'Didn't you tell me yourself Gair'd developed a bad back?' Patrick said. 'A slipped disc, I think you said. You said he had to have help in the garden nowadays. Digging a grave may have been beyond him, as well as something his gardener might have noticed. He may even have found the body too heavy to move any distance.'

She gave a sharp shudder, picked up the painting and carried it out of the room.

When she came back she said, 'I'll come over, if I may. If you're wrong it would be a pity if all those precious plants were lost. I'll heel them in and give them a chance to survive.'

'If that's what you want,' he said. 'It'll take some time. And if we find anything, you can leave before we have to uncover it.'

It was only then that the real meaning of what they had been talking about hit Valerie. Men were going to start digging in Charles's garden and were going to uncover Rhona's skeleton. Just a skeleton and perhaps a few rags and tatters of rotten clothing. That was all that would be left of her now, after five years.

Valerie gave a jerky little nod. 'Yes, I'll leave.'

Taking care that the dogs did not follow them out, she and Patrick let themselves out of the house.

The dogs at once began to whine at being left behind. The sound of it, pursuing Valerie as she crossed the courtyard, was so like the sound that had taken her to Charles's house on Sunday morning that it seemed to her a kind of warning of death. She felt sure now that the skeleton would be there under the *Androsace imbricata*, the *Daphne cneorum*, the *Dryas octopetala*. And to be thinking at all about the plants was fantastic. Of course, it was a refuge from thinking about those poor dry bones. And a good refuge, in its way. Pausing, she turned back to the toolshed and returned after a moment with a trowel and her gardening gloves. The men who had been waiting about near the cars joined her and Patrick at Charles's door, carrying picks and shovels.

Patrick unlocked the door and they went inside. The men tramped through the sitting-room and out through the french window into the garden beyond. The rockery was in a wide curve to the right of the window, very skilfully designed to simulate a natural outcrop of rock. Valerie remembered the strain of handling the lumps of stone, slithering them one by one into the positions that Charles had chosen for them, filling in the gaps between them with stone chippings and peat and sand, and enjoying herself more, while the two of them worked together, than she had since she had come here to live with Edmund. The weather had been fine and Charles had been gay and enthusiastic and apparently not in the least oppressed by the loss of his wife. Valerie remembered that that had puzzled her. To have tried to kill himself and only a few weeks later to be as lighthearted as a child on the seashore, building sand castles ...

One of the policemen had worked the tip of his pick under one of the rocks at the end of the rockery and loosened it. He and another man dragged it clear of soil and clinging plants and rolled it on to the lawn. Two other men went to work at the other end of the rockery. They hauled out stone after stone. The heap on the lawn grew. Patrick stood with his hands in his pockets, watching. Valerie stood beside him except when, from time to time, she darted forward to save some plant from under the boots of the men. She laid these on a separate heap which she planned to deal with later. Perhaps. Perhaps, when she left this garden, she would never want to return to it.

Suddenly quick footsteps sounded on the paving behind them.

'What the hell's going on?' a woman's voice demanded.

A voice that Valerie knew and which for a moment gave her a feeling of sick fright, as if a ghost had spoken. Then she turned to greet Rhona Gair.

Chapter 15

'This is Mrs Gair, Mr Dunn,' Valerie said. 'Rhona, this is Detective-Superintendent Dunn.'

Rhona gave him a little nod. She was a tall woman in her late thirties, erect, wide-shouldered, narrow-hipped, dressed in a suit of a soft burnt orange colour which looked both simple and expensive. She had black hair, smooth and shining as a helmet. Her eyes were blue, steady and rather steely. She was a very beautiful woman, Patrick realized, if you could face up to that look of a fighter about her, meet the challenge with which she faced you, the poised self-assertion.

'What are you doing to that rockery?' she asked him.

'As a matter of fact, Mrs Gair, we were looking for you,' he answered. 'We may as well discontinue the operation.' He called out to the men to stop their attack on the rockery. 'May I say I'm very glad to see you alive and well?'

'You thought you were going to find me under all that?' She nodded at what was left of the stones and the plants.

'We did,' he said.

'But why?'

'Because of what I thought was some very shrewd reasoning on my part. But for once I'm delighted to be wrong, even though it makes me out as more than a bit of a fool.'

Rhona Gair turned to Valerie. 'Hallo, Val. Nice to see you again after all these years. You haven't changed at all. Do you understand what this man's talking about?'

'More or less,' Valerie answered. 'He explained it to me. But I expect he'll want to explain it to you himself. Won't you, Mr Dunn?'

'Yes, now that you've appeared so opportunely, Mrs Gair,

I'd like to have a talk,' he said. 'If you don't mind, we can go into the house.'

'I'll go home then,' Valerie said. 'Come over, Rhona, if you want to when Mr Dunn's through with you. Come and have lunch.'

'Thank you, I will.'

The two women, Patrick noticed, were courteous but not cordial. After Valerie's first shock of relief at seeing Rhona Gair alive, neither had shown much pleasure at seeing one another again after all the years that had passed.

As soon as Valerie had gone Rhona turned back to him.

'You thought I was dead?'

'It seemed a fair enough assumption,' he said.

'And you were looking for me ... You thought Charles had killed me and put me there?'

'That was the idea.'

'I suppose you're going to explain it.'

Patrick was beginning to feel very tired of explaining his idea to people. He had had a long session of it first with the Chief Constable, then there had been Valerie Bayne, and now that the idea had turned out to be so mistaken he felt disinclined to talk about it at all. But he recognized that Rhona Gair had a certain right to know why the men here should be hunting in the garden for her dead body.

'Shall we go in?' he said. 'We can talk there.'

She led the way back into the sitting-room. It had been cleaned up by Mrs Jardine after the police had been through it. The grey film of fingerprint powder was gone. The fading flowers had been removed from the vases. Standing in the middle of the room, Rhona Gair looked slowly round her with what seemed an air of faint surprise, as if there were a strangeness about the very familiarity of the place.

'He hasn't changed anything,' she remarked. 'You know, I'd have thought he would have. We chose most of these things together, and enjoyed ourselves doing it. They stand for the best time in our marriage. I'd have expected him to want to blot it all out when I left. He was very angry with me about it, very, very angry. He couldn't bear not being the one who finally broke it up.'

Her calm was remarkable. If she had ever had strong feelings about her husband, whether loving him or hating him, they had long since died.

'How much do you know about what's happened here?' Patrick asked.

She strolled towards the piano and struck two or three notes at random, as if she wanted to be reminded of the sound of the instrument.

'Just what was in the papers,' she said. She reached for a silver cigarette box on the top of the piano, took out a cigarette and lit it with a lighter standing beside the box. Her hand had gone out automatically to both box and lighter, as if she had known just where they would be. 'I saw the bit on television too. I suppose it's the gruesome thing about that man in the cupboard that's got the murder all the publicity it's getting. We used to keep our gardening boots and gloves and things like that in the cupboard. I can't think what made Charles think of putting that Mexican into it.'

'My theory was that he had to put him somewhere in a hurry – or rather, that possibly that was what he'd had to do with another body on an earlier occasion, and that's when he found out the properties of the cupboard.'

They had both sat down.

'Another body – mine?' Rhona puffed out a long stream of smoke and laughed.

'Wasn't that quite likely?' Patrick said. 'You were expecting guests here, weren't you, the afternoon you left him? And if in fact you'd never got away because he'd been so angry with you that he'd killed you, he'd have had to hide you in a hurry and the cupboard would just about have had room for you. And you do seem to have vanished very completely straight away. I've asked around the people here, and no one seems to know what became of you. So I think my theory had quite a lot to be said for it.'

'I didn't vanish intentionally,' she said. 'I mean, I didn't do a deliberate vanishing trick. I just decided to go away and never come back. Actually I did come back once to collect some of my belongings, but I didn't see anyone around the place and it had an empty sort of feeling. I found out later it was because Charles was in hospital at the time, and I heard about his accident and that attempted suicide of his, which I could only conclude was because the accident had affected his brain, because he'd never have killed himself for love of me. And I went back to using my maiden name of Locksley and got a flat in Hampstead and a job working for an old friend of mine who's an outstanding photographer, and I cut all the old ties here. They weren't very strong. I was never very popular.' It was evident that that had not much concerned her. 'But you could have found me quite easily, I expect, if you'd looked for me.'

'If you saw no one when you came back that once,' Patrick said, 'how did you find out about your husband's accident and that suicide attempt?'

'From him,' she said. 'We wrote to each other a few times and talked on the telephone once or twice. We had to decide whether or not we were going to go ahead with a divorce, but in the end we didn't bother. Neither of us felt much drawn to a second marriage. And I didn't need any money from him. I've a certain amount of my own, apart from my job. So there were no property complications. It was all very straightforward really.'

'That final quarrel that made you decide to leave him – can you tell me what it was about?' Patrick asked.

'Oh, the usual thing,' she answered casually. 'His women. Actually it didn't begin as a quarrel. Suddenly I just couldn't think why I'd gone on putting up with the situation for so long and I told him I was leaving. Then, as I said, he got angry. He'd a very violent temper that flared up before you even knew what was happening. He started to threaten me and he picked up the poker. And perhaps it was only luck that he came to his senses and I'm not under the rockery.' She glanced towards the old fireplace. 'Where *is* the poker?'

'With a few odds and ends at the police station,' Patrick said. 'We found it lying under that chair you're sitting on, which seemed to us an odd place to keep a poker. So it seemed a good bet that it was the weapon that had been used to kill your husband. You probably know from the newspapers that he was killed by a blow on the head before he was hanged from that beam there to fake a suicide. But it turned out that the only fingerprints on the poker were his own.'

She looked thoughtfully up at the beam. Her expression was one of interest, not repulsion.

'So he probably picked it up to defend himself with, unless he was the attacker,' she said. 'Then I suppose it dropped out of his hand and rolled under here. Do you know what the weapon was that killed him?'

'We aren't sure,' Patrick answered. 'We think he could have been knocked backwards in a fight and hit his head against the fender and cracked his skull.'

'Would that be murder?'

'Just possibly not, if, as you suggest, he was the attacker. But remember he was hanged afterwards with a length of nylon clothes-line. That doesn't seem a very innocent act.'

'Perhaps whoever did it was in too much of a panic to think straight.' She flicked some ash from her cigarette into an ash-tray. 'Do you know the proverb, "Don't talk of halters in a hanged man's house"?'

'I think I've heard it.'

'I was just wondering if someone had been talking to him about something that hit one of his sore spots. He had plenty, of course, he was so vain. He couldn't stand the least breath of criticism. And if he'd lost his temper and grabbed the poker and hit out at whoever it was … But that brings us back to his having been hung up afterwards, doesn't it? Not a very helpful suggestion probably, though perhaps you might think about it.'

'Yes.' What Patrick was thinking about just then was that Rhona Gair, or Locksley, was a strongly built woman, taller than Gair by two or three inches, and that although he himself had said that the murder of Gair could not be a woman's crime, she was one who just possibly might have been capable of it. And perhaps she was ignorant enough to think that death caused by a violent blow on the head could be disguised as suicide by hanging. 'Now a question I must ask you, Mrs Gair – Miss Locksley – is what you were doing on Saturday evening. I've had to ask that of everyone who's had any connection with Dr Gair.'

'Naturally.' She took the question with her usual equanimity. 'Well, I was at home all the afternoon and evening.' She gave him the address of her London flat. 'The porter may have seen me come in soon after lunch, but he won't be able to say for certain whether or not I stayed in for the rest of the day. The man in charge of the garage may remember that I didn't take my car out, but of course if I'd had murder in mind I could have hired a car, couldn't I, or come down by train? So I haven't an alibi. But what I haven't either is a motive. My feelings about Charles have cooled. I didn't bear him any grudges. In fact, in a way, I'm quite grateful for the years I spent with him. At least they weren't dull. And I shan't gain financially by his death. He hadn't a great deal of money apart from his salary. This house belongs to the Martindale, of course, not to him, and he never tried to save money. So there are really just the odds and ends of furniture, some of which are pretty good and probably worth a reasonable amount at present day prices, but I'm certain he'll have made a will which makes sure I shan't get hold of any of it. For which I don't blame him. We made a clean break.'

'If the break was so complete, what made you feel you had to come here today?'

'Ah.' She took longer than usual to answer this, stubbing her cigarette out before she spoke, grinding it down in the ashtray with a force far beyond any that was necessary to extinguish it utterly. For the first time since she had appeared at Patrick's elbow in the garden she betrayed her tension.

'I told you, I read the news in the evening papers yesterday,' she said. 'And I saw the thing on television. At first I didn't know what to do. I didn't want to do anything. I didn't want to come. I didn't want to have anything to do with whatever had happened. That man in the cupboard – the cupboard where I told you we used to keep our boots and things – I couldn't

133

make any sense of it. So I tried to persuade myself that if I shut my eyes the problem would go away. Then I talked it over with Peter – Peter Cronshaw, the friend I work for, and yes, if you want to know about it, we've been lovers for a long time, though we've never actually tried living together. That would be too like marriage, of which we've each had some experience that didn't agree with us. And Peter advised me to come down here and introduce myself to the police, because otherwise it might look as if I were trying to hide. So I came, and if there are any more questions you want to ask me, I'm quite ready to go on answering them.'

Patrick was very aware of the challenge in her attitude, almost as if she were daring him to ask her anything more.

'Did they tell you at the police station you'd find me here,' he asked, 'or did you come straight here?'

'I came straight here, I'm not sure why.' She was sitting loungingly in her chair, relaxed and yet alert, with her long legs crossed and with her finely shaped, strong hands groping inside her bag for another cigarette. Patrick wondered why Charles Gair had not been satisfied with her. He would have found it difficult to find another woman as arrestingly beautiful. But had that been the trouble? Had he been unable to endure a relationship with a woman whom he could not easily dominate? He had gone in for being a striking personality himself, the sort of man people generally spoke of as a character. Had he been unable to accept the competition that she would have offered?

Lighting her second cigarette, she added, 'I just had an impulse to look at the place. There wasn't anything rational about it. Is there anything else you want to know?'

'Well, can you tell me where your husband normally kept his passport?'

'His *passport*?' She looked incredulous, as if she thought that perhaps she had not heard him correctly. 'Is that important?'

'I don't know about important, but at least it's odd,' Patrick answered.

'Why? ... Oh, is it something to do with that Mexican?'

'It could be. We haven't been able to find the passport, that's all, yet there are foreign coins in that writing table, which make it look as if he was in the habit of travelling.' Patrick gestured at the *bonheur du jour*. 'Anything odd could always turn out to be important, you understand.'

She nodded. 'Well, we used to keep both our passports in the top lefthand drawer there,' she said. 'But of course he may have altered his habits since I left him.'

'Did you travel much?'

'We generally had a holiday abroad once a year. Greece, Madeira, the Canaries, that sort of thing. Just the usual hunt for sunshine. And he sometimes went to conferences abroad.'

'Ever in Mexico?'

'No.'

'Did he ever speak of wanting to go to Mexico?'

'I don't remember. Perhaps. We were always making plans, most of which we never carried out. Anyway, we never went there.'

'And when you read the name Barragan in the newspaper, it meant nothing to you.'

'Not a thing.'

'Then there's just one thing more I want to ask,' Patrick said. 'It's about Mrs Rundell, who left her husband only a few days before you left yours. Was there any connection between those two events? Was she one of those women of his you referred to?'

He was prepared for her to flare up at the question, but she took it coolly, although perhaps her eyes grew a little brighter.

'I'd no proof of it, but I thought so,' she said.

'Had they a relationship that could have lasted over several years?' he asked.

'That would surprise me. Why?'

'It's only because of the way Mexico keeps cropping up at the moment. A dead Mexican in the cupboard in the cellar. Mexican coins in the drawer of the writing table. And a letter sent by Mrs Rundell to her husband from Mexico.'

She gave a curious abstracted smile, as if a thought had just crossed her mind which she did not intend to divulge.

'So you think Charles and Debbie Rundell met in Mexico for some reason,' she said, 'and Dr Barragan somehow got involved with them there – I see.' She contemplated the tip of her cigarette. Patrick suddenly felt completely convinced that she was concealing something, and thought how much easier it was for smokers than for non-smokers to hide their thoughts. There was always something that you could do with a cigarette, light it, draw on it, tip ash off it, stub it out or simply look at it, as this woman was doing now, which gave you a good reason for not looking your questioner in the face. 'But I can't help you. I know nothing about it.'

'Perhaps some idea may come to you, now that you're thinking about it,' he suggested.

'It's possible. If it does, I'll let you know. But I don't think it's likely.'

They both stood up.

'I'll go over to see Mrs Bayne and take her up on her invitation to lunch,' she said. 'If you want me, that's where you'll find me.'

With Patrick opening doors for her, she went out and walked away across the courtyard.

He returned to the sitting-room and went to the french window, standing there looking out at the group of men who were squatting on the heap of stones that they had unearthed from the rockery. They were looking very well content to rest there in the bright morning sunshine. Their picks and shovels lay about on the lawn. The rockery itself looked like a gaping wound ruthlessly hacked open in the fine, firm green of the pleasant garden.

Sergeant Farley was there, standing with his broad back to the house, chatting to the men and unaware of Patrick at the window. He looked out at them with a kind of anger smouldering in his eyes. To have had one of your brighter ideas shown up as absurd is enough to make any man angry, particularly if you are beginning to feel haunted by a feeling that trickery has been involved somewhere, that you are thinking precisely as you have been meant to think, that some trap has been sprung on you into which you should never have been such a fool as to blunder, open-eyed. Not that Patrick could have said why he had that feeling. Perhaps it was only one of the side-effects of humiliation, of the thought of those men out there having their laugh at the way he had made a fool of himself.

After a moment he gave a shrug and walked forward into the garden. Farley heard him and turned.

'What now, sir?' he asked. 'Do they leave things as they are or try to put things back? They may make a pretty good mess of it. There isn't a man here, myself included, who hasn't been trained to deliver a baby, but we aren't landscape gardeners.'

'No,' Patrick said. 'Go on.'

'Go *on*?' Farley said. 'Go on taking the rockery apart?'

'That's right. And dig down under it. Dig very carefully. See that they do that – dig very carefully. Now I'm going into Keyfield. I'm going to the Rundell house, then I'll be in my office. If you find anything, call me at once.'

'If you'd tell us what we're looking for, now that that lady's walked in alive and well – '

'You'll know what it is, if you find it,' Patrick said.

He turned back into the house, went through it, out into the courtyard and walked quickly to his car.

Chapter 16

At the Rundells' house he found Isobel at home, and when, in her long droopy dress and wooden clogs, she took him into the prim, drab sitting-room, he found both Ivor Haydon and Alberti Barragan sitting there. They and Isobel were all having drinks and were smoking. Isobel offered Patrick a drink too, at which, when he declined, Ivor gave a sardonic laugh.

'You don't drink with suspects, do you?' he said. He had stood up with reluctant courtesy when Patrick entered, but his manner was aggressive.

'More often than you'd think,' Patrick said. 'After all, who's to know what suspicions one's got in one's head? But I don't often drink when I'm working.'

'Do you wish to be private?' Alberti Barragan asked in his solemn way. 'Do you wish us to leave?'

'Don't think of it,' Isobel said quickly. 'You're staying for lunch, remember. That's why I've been bothering with all that salad and stuff. If it was just going to be my father and me I'd have made sandwiches. If Mr Dunn wants to talk to me privately we can go into the dining-room. Is it anything private, Mr Dunn?' She looked as if she half-hoped that it was, though she did not want to risk letting her guests abandon her.

'Not in the least,' Patrick said. 'And if you like it can wait till your father gets home. Will he be coming home for lunch? I hoped I might find him here.'

'I don't think he'll be back till the evening,' Isobel said. 'But what is it? Can't I help?'

She had sat down and with her long skirt, her glass in one hand and cigarette in the other, managed to look quite unlike the schoolgirl whom Patrick had seen the day before.

'I'm interested in the letters your mother wrote to your

father since she left him,' he said. 'Am I right that there were several?'

'Yes,' Isobel said. 'But why in the world ...?' She looked at him with a puzzled frown. 'Why are you interested in her at all?'

'It's obvious,' Ivor said. 'It's because of that letter from Mexico. It has to tie in somehow.'

'But there was nothing in that letter,' Isobel said. 'Nothing special.'

'Have you got it?' Patrick asked.

'Yes, we kept all her letters,' Isobel answered. 'I – I missed her so at first, I used to keep on taking them out and reading them, though they were funny letters in a way. They never told one anything. And then, well, it became a sort of habit to keep them. When a new one came, I just added it to the others. So they're all there. Do you want to see them?'

'I do, if you don't mind,' Patrick said, 'and I'd like to take them away with me. But that's something I probably ought to ask your father about.'

Persuading a girl of Isobel's age to let him take those letters away with him was something that might get him into trouble.

But she said, 'Oh, he wouldn't mind. He'd have thrown them away if I hadn't saved them.'

'There's something else,' Patrick went on. 'Have you anything she wrote before she went away?'

Her puzzled frown came back. 'What sort of thing?'

'Anything. Your name written in a book she gave you. An old shopping list. A diary. Anything at all that you know she wrote.'

'There's an old diary – well, I don't mean a diary that tells you anything about her, but an appointment book with notes about whom she was going to have lunch with and so on. Will that do?'

'Excellently.'

She stood up. 'I'll get them.'

As she went out Ivor gave another of his sardonic laughs.

'This case is getting more and more fantastic,' he said. 'What do you expect to find in an old diary?'

'I'm simply checking on every angle,' Patrick answered.

'Not you. You're following some quite definite line of thought.'

'I wish I were.' Having made a fool of himself recently, Patrick was not going to admit to anyone that he had definite thoughts about anything. Yet the fact was, logic was logic, and perhaps he had not been quite as much of a fool as he must have looked.

'Is it not a tragic thing,' Alberti Barragan said, 'the way this young girl has treasured everything of her mother's? If her mother had understood how it would be, do you think she would have gone away and left her?'

'Well, if you were married to a dry stick like Rundell,' Ivor said, 'do you think you could have stuck around for ever, even for the sake of your daughter? And Debbie Rundell seems to have been quite a woman, the way they all talk about her still around the Martindale, even after all these years. She seems to have been about the most exciting thing that ever happened to them. But she must have found it just about the end. All the same –' He looked intently at Patrick. 'You won't find anything wrong with those books you're examining. I don't know why you're wasting your time with them. Rundell's a bonehead, but he's dead honest.'

'I'm simply checking on every angle,' Patrick said again. 'Which reminds me, Dr Haydon, when that alibi of yours broke down, you didn't exactly stick to the truth in what you told us next, did you?'

Ivor grinned. 'What was I to do? In my place, wouldn't you have tried to cover up for Isobel?'

'In spite of the fact that she'd let you down about the evening? Didn't she break a date with you when she got Gair's invitation?'

'Yes, and that irritated me a bit, but it didn't break my heart. And when I realized that she might be in serious trouble if the truth came out, I did my best to cover up for her. I don't mean I was worrying about what you thought, but I didn't want her father knowing what was going forward with Gair.'

'He knows now,' Patrick said. 'She told him herself.'

'How did he take it?'

'Very quietly.'

'He would. He takes everything quietly. It doesn't mean he won't take it out on her in his own fashion.'

'What is his own fashion?'

'I'd say it's to withhold the affection the poor kid needs so badly. Though God knows, perhaps he doesn't do it intentionally. Perhaps he simply hasn't any affection to give, or else doesn't know how to give what he has. And at least she's got one good thing out of the business. He's let her leave school. A sensible decision in her case, I'd say. She wasn't getting much out of going there.'

'Of course you realize that her changing her story about Saturday evening means you haven't much of an alibi yourself,' Patrick said. 'There are the gramophone records your landlady heard, but that can be rigged.'

Ivor grinned again. But one of his feet began to tap the floor.

'And I'm a clever fellow, so I could easily have rigged it, couldn't I?' he said. It seemed to Patrick that there was a hint of effort behind the mockery in his tone. 'Have you found out why I wanted to kill Gair?'

'I've been getting the feeling recently that just knowing Gair might have made anyone want to kill him,' Patrick answered. 'Apart from that, you could have taken it amiss that he'd stolen your girl, and from what I've heard, that he wasn't going to renew your job here.'

Ivor looked him gravely in the face for a moment, as if to make sure whether or not he was serious.

'I thought you understood Isobel isn't my girl in any important sense,' he said. 'I'm fond of the kid, I like her company. But if she preferred Gair to me, that was that. It worried me a bit, I confess. If things went ahead between them, she was going to get hurt. But then I thought, she's got to grow up some time and most people get hurt one way or another when that's happening to them, so why try to interfere? I wouldn't have thought of running my neck into a noose for her sake.'

'A noose?' Alberti Barragan said with interest. 'I was under the impression capital punishment had been stopped in this country.'

'I was speaking figuratively,' Ivor said. 'Using an idiom. Not that our friend here probably doesn't regret the fact that we've given up the noose. The police are all for hanging, aren't they, Superintendent? You'd bring it back if you could.'

Patrick, whose private opinion was that if hanging were ever reintroduced then all adult members of the community, including women, should be liable for execution service, just as they were for jury service, and not have their murderous duty carried out for them anonymously by a public servant, did not feel like entering on a discussion of the point with Ivor Haydon. But a thought connected with what Ivor had just said came into his mind, slid out of it and disappeared before he could grasp it. The feeling of this worried him. What had it been? Something to do with hanging, of course, with Gair ...

'And what about your job here?' he asked. 'Does that mean any more to you than Miss Rundell?'

Before Ivor could answer, Alberti Barragan broke in, 'I tell you, if I knew a girl like that, so young, so ignorant of life, were going to be seduced by a man like this Dr Gair, even if I were not in love with her, I would have been prepared to kill him with my own hands. He must have been a fiend, this man, a devil.'

Ivor's mocking smile reappeared. 'Are you sure you didn't kill him with those hands of yours anyway?' he asked. 'You'd a better reason than anyone else. My job, incidentally, Superintendent, is something I was getting ready to turn in anyway. There are no prospects here. It's a dead end. I want to get abroad as soon as I can.'

'I had a reason, yes, but I did not know I had a reason,' Barragan said gravely. 'If I had known of my father's death, of the manner of it, I could have killed Dr Gair myself. I have already said this. I would have killed him with my own hands.'

'Those hands,' Ivor murmured. 'You'd better learn to keep them under control.'

'Pardon?'

142

'Never mind. Go on. I suppose you really didn't know of your father's death. I can't help wondering about that. After all, Gair and your father must have had some connection in Mexico. That's self-evident. And suppose you were in on it too, whatever it was, so that when your father disappeared in England you guessed straight away Gair must be at the bottom of it.'

'And I waited a year, a whole year, to take revenge for it?' Barragan said with scorn. 'This is idiocy.'

'Well, suppose the evidence against Gair only came into your hands recently,' Ivor went on, looking as if he enjoyed goading the other young man, 'perhaps through Mrs Rundell, who of course is tied in with it somewhere – '

He was interrupted again, this time by the clatter of Isobel's wooden soles in the hall and the door opening.

She had an envelope in her hand and a small notebook.

'Here they are,' she said, handing them to Patrick. 'The letters and the diary. It's for the year before she went away. There isn't much in it. Just notes for appointments for hair-dos and the dentist and meeting her friends. There isn't anything there that tells you anything about her, if that's what you were hoping for. That's in the letters. Only, as I said, they're funny letters for her to have bothered to write, because they never really told us anything about her or gave us an address to write back to. I think my father believed they meant she didn't want to break the tie with us completely, and was going to come back some day, but I don't know – I used to think that too when I was a child, only now, after five years, it doesn't seem to make sense any more. Do you think it does?'

'Perhaps I'll know more about that when I've looked at the letters,' Patrick said. 'Thank you, anyway. I'd better give you a receipt for them.'

He took a notebook out of his pocket and wrote the receipt.

'You'll let me have them back, won't you?' Isobel said anxiously.

'Oh yes.' But privately he wondered if she would want them back when he was finished with them. If he was not again being the clumsiest sort of fool, she might find that she thought

143

of them with a kind of hatred. 'But I'll probably be keeping them for a day or two at least.'

'Yes – all right – but be careful of them.'

He promised to be careful and went away, leaving her to organize her little lunch party.

He had his own lunch in the Green Man, then went to the police station. In his room he leafed through the diary, then glanced at the letters, but did not bother to read them. Instead he picked up the telephone and after a few minutes' conversation with another department in the building, sent for a constable to take the letters and the diary over to it. He had done as little explaining as he could about what he wanted, but after all, the question that he wanted answered was a quite simple one. He did not think that it would provide much of a problem to a skilled man.

Yet after the letters and diary were out of his hands, he had a sharp attack of misgiving. Sitting at his desk for some minutes, staring at the blank wall opposite him, he cursed himself for being possessed of an imagination. You were hardly ever complimented or even liked for having one. Not that you would really have been prepared to part with your gift, if that was what the thing was. All the same, it often exposed you to disconcerting hazards.

He wondered if it would be different if you worked in a place like the Martindale, instead of the police. Or would it be just the same? Probably just the same, he thought, even if there was a little more gloss on the surface, a little more sophistication to cover up the averageness underneath. Not that Gair had been average, and Patrick suspected that Edmund Hackett had as much imagination as was good for him, and probably his sister had too.

Her image came vividly into Patrick's mind at the moment. He also thought of Rhona Gair. She was very much the more beautiful of the two women, yet he felt an odd kind of satisfaction with himself for being able to recognize that there was a subtlety in the charm of Valerie Bayne which was lacking in the other woman and that he was capable of being far more moved by that quality of hers that was not exactly beauty than he was by anything in Rhona Gair. He would never dream the briefest dream about Rhona.

His thoughts came to an abrupt stop. He switched them sharply off Valerie. Standing up so abruptly that his chair scraped noisily on the floor, he left his room, walked out to his car and drove back to the Martindale.

In Charles Gair's garden the dismantling of the rockery had continued, according to Patrick's orders. The pile of rocks near it had grown, with another heap beside it of plants probably irremediably damaged by their uprooting. But at the moment when Patrick walked out through the french window to join the men around the gaping scar of loose soil and gravel, there was no activity going on. All of them were standing round the hole that they had dug in attitudes of curiously arrested movement. They seemed to have been taken by surprise, all as stiffly still as if they had been standing at attention.

Farley saw Patrick.

'Well, she's here, sir,' the sergeant said.

'She?' Patrick said.

He went to the edge of the hole and looked in.

'Yes,' he answered himself.

He did not need Dr Inglis to tell him that the skeleton that the police had uncovered was that of a woman. Tatters of clothing still clung to the bare bones. Nylon does not decay much even after years of burial in the earth. And there was a chain of gold links that had fallen loosely about the bones of the neck, and ear-rings lying on each side of the skull. The gold of them was dull, but its yellowness showed through the clinging soil.

'Yes,' Patrick said again, 'there she is. That's as far as she ever actually travelled.'

'There's something there beside her,' Farley said. 'We haven't touched it, but to me it looks uncommonly like a knife. And what's a bit queer about it, it's done up in plastic.'

Chapter 17

Rhona Gair and Valerie had had lunch together and over their sherry, omelettes, salad and cheese Rhona had told Valerie much the same about herself as she had just told Patrick Dunn.

Valerie's response to it had been subdued. Rhona had always overpowered her. The tall woman's self-possession had always produced the shyness in Valerie of a girl years younger than she was. And even after five years, during which she had done a good deal of maturing, she had the feeling of being reduced in scale by Rhona, made a little shadowy and insignificant.

Yet Rhona had always been friendly and presumably could not help it if she happened to have more personality, more vitality than most people. Drinking coffee, sitting in a low chair, with her long legs stretched out before her with the shapely ankles crossed, she chain-smoked and chatted quietly about herself.

'D'you know, it's an extraordinarily uncomfortable feeling having someone digging up the grave you're supposed to be in?' she said. 'It isn't as funny as you'd think. It gave me gooseflesh. I wish I'd arrived in time to stop them getting started.'

'It's a pity they've spoilt the rockery for nothing,' Valerie said. 'So many rockeries are pretty horrible things, but that one was a beauty. It fitted so naturally into its place.'

Rhona laughed. 'I never saw it in its prime. Charles only got it started after I'd left him. And I needn't pretend to worry about it. The house wasn't ours. It'll be handed over to the new Director, whoever he is. Charles really did his gardening for him. Who d'you think it'll be?'

Valerie shook her head. 'I don't know.'

'Will it be Edmund?'

'He says it's unlikely. He says, for one thing, he wouldn't be keen to take the job, even if it was offered to him. He's got enough administration already.'

'That's what Charles always used to say. He used to curse the amount he had to do, but of course he couldn't have borne not to be a Director or a professor or something. He could never have stood working under anybody else. D'you know, I can't get used to the idea that he's dead? I always envisaged him turning into one of those small, gnome-like, explosive old men, who outlive everyone they know and have more and more legends clinging to them and whose names are never mentioned without reverential sort of laughs, as if, of course, they're terrific jokes and yet so wonderful. I can hardly believe that isn't going to happen to him. Perhaps I would if I'd actually seen him dead, but I haven't, so it just seems unreal.'

'He wasn't a pretty sight,' Valerie said.

'No, of course he wasn't – I'm sorry – stupid of me,' Rhona said. 'I'd forgotten it was you who found him. Valerie, what do you honestly think is the explanation of it all?'

'I've stopped trying to guess,' Valerie answered.

'But you've been here all this time. You and Edmund knew Charles as well as anyone did. Haven't you any idea about how it happened?'

There was no grief in the way that Rhona spoke of Charles, but there was very real curiosity.

Valerie shook her head again. 'We're as much at sea as anyone. That man in the cupboard was just a ghastly shock. I haven't the beginnings of an explanation of what he was doing there.'

Rhona emptied her coffee cup and set it down.

'I can tell you one thing from my knowledge of my dear Charles,' she said. 'I bet he got a hell of a kick out of having the man there. I don't know how he found out that things didn't decay in that cupboard. Perhaps he'd found a dead rat in it, or something like that, that hadn't decayed. But once the poor Mexican chap was in it, Charles would have been thrilled to bits at having him there in the house. He was a bit of a collector as you know. Furniture and stuff. And a mummified man would have been quite the most precious thing in his collection. Only, of course, he couldn't have shown him off to anyone, which would have taken some of the fun out of it, one would suppose.'

'How you hated him, didn't you, Rhona?' Valerie said.

Rhona leant her handsome dark head against the back of the chair and looked meditatively at Valerie.

'I didn't love him. Except at first. But how I loved him then, the ugly little bastard. That made it all the worse later on, when I found out how little I meant to him. I was vain, I suppose. I'd been spoiled. I didn't believe I couldn't make a man love me if I wanted him to. And so all the love I had for him turned into something . . .' She caught her breath. 'Yes, you're quite right, I hated him by the time I left him. But I didn't kill him, if that's what's on your mind. What do you think, are the police going to think I did?'

'I believe they've decided it couldn't have been a woman's crime,' Valerie said.

'But I'm a rather strong woman.' Rhona lit another of her swiftly smoked cigarettes. 'Oh God, I hope they aren't going to try to mix me into all this. Life was so bloody for such a long time before I settled down with Peter, and now it's so good. I don't want it ruined. Is that selfish? I expect it is. But the way I look at it is this. I wasn't selfish enough when I ought to have been, so now I've got a right to be.' She turned her head at the sound of footsteps. 'Is that Edmund, or is it the police coming after me?'

It was Edmund, accompanied by Hugh.

Edmund exclaimed in surprise at seeing Rhona, but though he clasped her hand and shook it warmly, there was dismay in his eyes, as if the presence of Charles's wife could only make a complicated situation more complicated. Hugh gave her only a brief handshake and an abstracted smile, as if he were not certain that he remembered who she was, but hoped to keep this covered up. Actually it was impossible that he should have forgotten her. They had known each other for years and she had altered very little in appearance since he had seen her last. But he seemed to find it difficult to bring his thoughts back from whatever place it was to which they had retreated and to be reluctant to pay any attention to the people in the room.

'I suppose it oughtn't to be a surprise, seeing you, Rhona,' Edmund said. 'Of course it was natural you'd come once our news got into the papers. Or did anyone here get in touch with you?'

'No, I haven't been in touch with anyone at the Martindale for years,' she answered. 'I saw it in my evening paper.'

'Anyway, it's nice to see you again,' he said. 'You're looking splendid.'

'How did you think I'd be looking?' she asked. 'Dead?'

'Dead?' he said, puzzled.

'That's what the police thought I was going to turn out to be until I walked in alive,' she told him. 'They were hunting for me under Charles's rockery. I think seeing me was a bit of a blow to that detective. He thought he'd got on to something really interesting.'

'I don't understand,' Hugh said. 'Why should anyone think you were dead? It sounds most extraordinary.'

'Just that I haven't been around lately,' she answered.

'And, you see,' Valerie said, 'the Superintendent thinks Dr Barragan may not have been the first body that went into that cupboard.'

'And of course, husbands and wives kill each other more often than they kill anyone else,' Edmund said. 'Is there any of that coffee left, Val? Hugh and I have been talking to Speight all the morning and it's been a bit of a strain. He couldn't make up his mind whether he believed Hugh had murdered Charles because Charles had caught him fiddling the books, or whether it was impossible for anyone at the Martindale to have committed any sort of crime. Anyway, to show solidarity, the three of us went out to lunch together, but it was heavy going. Fortunately, the old boy's on his way back to London now, and I don't think is anxious to get mixed up in things here more than he has to.'

'I'll make some more coffee,' Valerie said, and picking up the coffee-pot, went out to the kitchen.

She was grinding the coffee when Hugh appeared in the doorway.

He spoke in a low voice, as if he were afraid that what he said could be heard in the sitting-room. 'What's she really come for, Val? It isn't like her to get more involved than she's got to.'

'She hasn't said much about it,' Valerie said, 'but I suppose she thought it was only proper, as Charles's wife, to put in an appearance.'

'Rhona's never cared much about what was proper.'

'Well, I can't think of any other reason for her to come.'

'No, but I still feel uneasy about it. If she thought she ought to make some statement to the police, she could have phoned them and let someone interview her in London. But Rhona's always given me an uncomfortable sort of feeling. "By the pricking of my thumbs, something wicked this way comes . . ." I don't quite mean that, of course. I was entirely on her side when she left Charles. All the same, in medieval times I'd have been all in favour of having her burnt as a witch.'

Valerie laughed. 'I can't think of any reason why she should have come except to tell the police what she can. And perhaps just a bit out of curiosity to see what's going on. Have you seen Isobel since the morning, by the way? I met her in Keyfield with Dr Barragan – the son – we had coffee together, and she told me you'd taken her away from school.'

'Do you think I was wrong?' Hugh asked. 'I thought it was the only thing I could do now. If it came out that she'd been going alone to the house of a man like Gair and getting herself involved in a murder, the school might not be all that anxious to keep her. So I thought it would be better to keep her at home before things started to come out at the inquest. Apart from that – oh, I don't know, Val. She's never cared much for me. I've never been able to do the right thing for her. She's resented my keeping her at school all this past year. So I thought, why not let her have her way, as I usually do, and if no good comes of it, well . . .' He shrugged his shoulders.

Valerie poured boiling water over the coffee in the filter.

'Taking her away was probably the only thing you could do,' she said.

'You don't think I've simply given in to her too easily? I nearly always give in to her, you know. I put up a show of resistance, then I crumple up. I can't stand her hatred. Because she does get into moods of really hating me when I oppose her. And that reminds me so of the moods Debbie used to get into during the months before she left me, quiet furies that were meant to make me feel I was the lowest thing on earth, that I'd always do anything to get her out of it. I'm very spineless. Perhaps I ought to have made Isobel stay at school and take the consequences of her actions.'

'They'd probably have gone to her head pretty badly,' Valerie said, putting cups on a tray. 'Think of the glamour of it. She'd probably have been the envy of every girl in the school.'

He smiled uncertainly. 'Perhaps it's lucky that didn't occur to her.'

He followed Valerie back to the sitting-room.

They found Rhona and Edmund chatting about photography, as if such a thing as the gruesome death of Rhona's husband had never taken place. She was telling him about the work of her friend, Peter Cronshaw, who specialized in portraits of children and also ran a sideline in alpine flowers. He had a book of these coming out shortly. She obviously took far more interest in his work than she ever had in Charles's. But there was one similarity in her attitude to both men. As Valerie remembered it, it had always been extremely important to Rhona to have Charles recognized as extraordinarily brilliant, and now she was anxious to impress them all with the fact that her lover was equally gifted. She was one of those women who cannot see herself as loving a man who does not seem markedly superior to most others. She was still talking enthusiastically about the book on alpine flowers when there was a knock at the door.

This time it was Isobel, accompanied by Ivor Haydon and Alberti Barragan.

Isobel came in quickly, her wooden clogs thumping on the floor, ignored everyone in the room but Hugh, ran to him and clutched at his arms with both hands.

'Daddy, I think I've done something awful!' she cried in a scared voice. 'I didn't mean to. I didn't think of what I was doing. It was only afterwards I started thinking, and now – I don't know, but I'm sure I should never have done it.'

Hugh disengaged himself stiffly from her grasp, embarrassed by this display in front of so many people.

'What have you done?' he asked in his level voice.

'I gave that policeman Mummy's letters.'

'You gave ...? That man Dunn? He asked for them?' Hugh sounded shaken.

'Yes, and I know, I *know* I should have refused. They were all written to you, after all. I'd no right to give them away. And it was only after he took them away that I started wondering why he wanted them. It's because he wants to involve Mummy in things, isn't it? And you wouldn't want that, would you? I know you wouldn't.'

Rhona interrupted, 'Hugh, is this your Isobel?'

Holding his daughter off at arm's length, Hugh muttered, 'Yes.'

'Oh God, how the young make one feel one's age!' Rhona said. 'She was a child when I went away. A little girl. And now she's a woman. A very beautiful one. The image of Debbie. Do you know how like your mother you are, Isobel?'

Isobel gave her a blank, unfriendly stare and did not answer.

Rhona's voice sharpened. 'Don't you know who I am? Have I changed so much?'

'Oh no, you're Charles's wife,' Isobel answered indifferently. 'Daddy, about giving that man those letters, was it an awful thing to do? Does it matter?'

'Just a minute,' Edmund said, looking with a worried frown from father to daughter. 'Can you tell us exactly what happened, Isobel? Dunn came and asked you for them, did he?'

She turned to Ivor. 'You tell them,' she said.

'Barragan and I were there,' Ivor said. 'We saw it all. Dunn simply asked for the letters, he didn't say why, and Isobel gave them to him without any hesitation, and he gave her a receipt for them. It was only afterwards she began to think she'd had no right to give them away like that and wanted to tell you about it.' He turned to Hugh. 'So we went to the Station to look for you and were told you'd been seen walking away with Dr Hackett. So we came looking for you here.'

'You haven't told him about the diary,' Isobel said.

'Oh, yes, the diary,' Ivor went on. 'Dunn asked if Isobel had anything her mother had written before she went away, and she said she had a diary, and she got it with the letters and gave them to him.'

There was a little silence in the room, as if everyone there were taking in the meaning of what had happened and all their faces became oddly alike, all touched by fear.

Then Edmund said harshly, 'Couldn't you have stopped her, Ivor? You and Barragan, you're not children.'

'I am sorry, sir,' Barragan said. 'I was disturbed at what was happening, but as a stranger in the house, as a foreigner, I did not feel it was for me to interfere.'

'No, of course not,' Edmund said. 'I ought not to have blamed you. But you, Ivor – not that I suppose it matters. Hugh would have given Dunn the letters if he'd been asked for them. Wouldn't you, Hugh? It doesn't really make any difference.'

He seemed in a hurry to smooth over his sudden eruption of anger.

Hugh was looking dazed. 'I don't understand,' he said. 'Yes, I'd have given him the letters if he'd asked me for them. Don't worry about it, Isobel. Why should anyone worry? There was nothing in those letters that anyone need worry about. I don't know about the diary. I didn't even know Debbie kept a diary.'

'It wasn't a real diary,' Isobel said. 'It was only a little notebook in which she wrote down her appointments for the next few weeks.'

'I wonder if any of them were with Charles,' Rhona said. 'That might interest the police. But if they were with Charles, I dare say she'd have had a private code for them. What do you think, Hugh? Would even Debbie have made a simple entry in her diary that she'd a date with Charles?'

'Cut it out, Rhona,' Edmund said. 'Hugh's got enough on his mind already.'

'I simply don't understand,' Hugh repeated confusedly. He

walked unsteadily to a chair and dropped into it. 'Everything seems to have gone mad these last few days. From the time Debbie's letter came on Saturday. From Paris. There wasn't anything in it that meant anything, any more than there was in any of the others. It made me wish she wouldn't go on and on writing, but would just leave me alone. And then next day we found Charles dead and that man – Dr Barragan – in the cupboard. And now they're even looking at the books of the Martindale. That doesn't worry me. They won't find anything wrong with them. But then it turns out Isobel was the woman Charles was expecting to dinner, and I've said to her, "All right, leave school, if that's what you want," – I've tried to do my best for her and for everyone all round, but that doesn't seem to amount to anything . . .' His words were blurring, as if he were drunk.

Rhona observed him coolly. 'You know, I believe he *is* afraid of what they may find in those letters,' she said.

'Damn it, leave him alone!' Edmund exclaimed. 'He's had as much as he can stand.' He strode to the drinks cupboard, poured out some whisky and took it to Hugh. 'Here, try some of this.'

As Hugh took hold of it fumblingly, Isobel went close to him again and put a hand on his shoulder.

'Daddy, I'm so sorry – so sorry about everything,' she said. 'Charles and all, I mean. I know I've been awful. But I didn't mean anything. And giving that man those letters, I just didn't know you'd mind.'

Hugh caught hold of her hand and held on to it tightly.

'I don't. It doesn't matter. I just don't understand – '

There was another knock at the door.

Again, there was an abrupt little silence. Again, there was a flicker of fear across two or three faces in the room. Then Edmund went rapidly to the door and opened it.

Patrick Dunn stood there, with Sergeant Farley beside him.

Chapter 18

'Good afternoon, Dr Hackett,' Patrick said. 'I was told at the research station I'd find you and Mr Rundell here. And I believe Mrs Bayne and Mrs Gair are here too. And I see you've got Miss Rundell and Dr Haydon and Dr Barragan here as well. That's very convenient. I've something I want to show you all. May we come in?'

Edmund did not answer, but opened the door wider for them to enter.

The two detectives advanced a little way into the room. Patrick thrust a hand into his breast pocket and brought out two plastic envelopes. In one was a necklace, in the other a pair of ear-rings. Earth still clung to the pieces of jewellery, but the gold of which they were made shone through it with a dull yellow gleam. Patrick held out the envelopes, one on the palm of each hand, first to Hugh.

'Do you recognize these?' Patrick said.

Hugh's eyes were blank, as if he could not see properly.

'I don't remember . . .' he muttered.

'Look carefully,' Patrick said. 'Think.'

Hugh went on looking at the envelope with the same empty stare and did not answer.

Patrick held out his hands so that the others could see what he was holding.

'Does anyone recognize these?'

Isobel gave a cry. 'Daddy, they're Mummy's! You remember – you must remember! You gave them to her.'

Hugh closed his eyes and swayed in his chair.

Patrick returned the envelopes to his pockets.

'Mr Rundell, how long have you known that your wife's letters were forgeries?' he asked.

It was a moment before Hugh would open his eyes to look at his interrogator. Then he repeated, as if it were the only sentence that he had learnt in a foreign language, 'I don't understand.'

'None of us understands,' Edmund said. 'What are you telling us, Mr Dunn?'

'That we went on digging under the rockery in Dr Gair's garden after Mrs Gair came over here,' Patrick answered, 'and that there was a skeleton there, even though it wasn't Mrs Gair's. And these things, this necklace and these ear-rings, were there with the bones. Mr Rundell, your daughter's just identified them as her mother's. Do you confirm that?'

'Yes,' Hugh said almost inaudibly. 'I didn't recognize them at first. I couldn't believe, couldn't make any sense of it. But I gave them to her a year or two before she left me and she seemed to like them, she wore them a lot. Are you telling me she's dead? *She's* the skeleton?'

'But how can she be?' Isobel blurted out. 'We had a letter from her only on Saturday.'

Hugh raised a hand to silence her. 'That's what you're telling us, isn't it, Mr Dunn?'

'We haven't made any formal identification yet,' Patrick said. 'But it's clear the body was buried wearing this necklace and the ear-rings, and if they were your wife's, it suggests that the skeleton is probably hers. However, there's some dental work that will have to be checked before it can be said for certain.'

'Dead,' Hugh muttered. 'I've thought all sorts of things about Debbie – horrible things, some of them. I've thought she was a crook. I've thought she was a whore. I've wanted her to be dead. Then again, I've wanted her to come back to us. I've believed everything could be put right. But that she's been dead all this time, that's the one thing I'd never thought of.'

Edmund had pushed chairs forward for Patrick and the sergeant to sit on.

'But about those letters, how do you explain them?' he asked.

'They're forgeries, Dr Hackett,' Patrick answered as he sat

down. 'Clumsy forgeries. Comparing them with the writing in the diary, which is known to be Mrs Rundell's, it took our expert only a very short time to come up with that answer. Someone wanted to keep the fiction going that Mrs Rundell was alive. And the question is, Mr Rundell, how long have you known that?'

Hugh had covered his face with his hands. He gave a small moan through his fingers.

'I never even thought of it,' he said. 'I never suspected anything.'

'Can't you explain to us how this has all come out, Mr Dunn?' Edmund said. Somehow he had achieved an air of authority in the room, as if he were responsible for all the people there. 'You didn't start digging in that rockery by chance.'

'Yes, well, I can explain,' Patrick replied, 'though most of it will come out at the inquest and you'll all have to be there. That'll be on Thursday afternoon. Yes, Mrs Gair?'

Rhona had made a sound of hasty protest, as if at having to stay on in Keyfield for so long, but as he looked at her she shook her head. 'No, go on,' she said.

'It began,' he said, 'with my starting to puzzle over what seemed to me one of the most fantastic incidents in the case, that attempted suicide of Dr Gair's when he was in hospital after his accident. There seemed to be no doubt that the attempt was genuine, yet from everything I'd heard about him, it seemed quite out of character. He didn't seem to have had the passionate and exclusive sort of love for his wife which would make suicide likely simply because she'd left him. And as soon as he got home from the hospital, he appeared to have become quite cheerful and to have developed a great interest in building a rockery in his garden. There was also the fact that I couldn't believe that Dr Gair had put Dr Barragan's body in the cupboard in the cellar without some prior knowledge that it would be preserved there. And how could he have had that knowledge? Only by experiment, I thought – if he'd put another body in the cupboard once before and it had been preserved. And the body that seemed most likely to me was Mrs Gair's.

None of you had seen her since she left her husband. She seemed to have vanished into thin air.'

He smiled faintly at Rhona.

'I've been in trouble before for jumping to conclusions,' he said. 'Sometimes it pays to risk it, sometimes you have to suffer for it. This time I happened to jump to the wrong conclusion. Yet not as wrong as all that. Even though Mrs Gair was alive, I still felt my basic reasoning was sound, that Dr Gair had had a body on his hands which he bundled into the cupboard because he was expecting guests, that he tried to kill himself in the hospital because he was expecting to be arrested for murder, and that when that didn't happen, and he discovered what had actually happened to the body, he set about burying it under a new rockery.'

'And I helped him!' Valerie exclaimed. 'A lot of those stones were heavy. We moved them together. He wasn't very strong yet after his accident and he let me help him!'

'But how did you work it out that you'd find Mrs Rundell there?' Ivor asked.

'Because I went on believing someone *had* to be there,' Patrick said. 'I was sure of my reasoning. And Mrs Rundell was another missing woman. She was just as missing as Mrs Gair, except for those letters of hers that kept coming from all over the world. Rather odd letters, I was given to understand, that never really told anyone anything about herself, or gave an address where she could be contacted. So I began to wonder if something was wrong with the letters. If Mrs Rundell was dead, then of course they had to be forgeries. It had to be that someone, probably Dr Gair himself, was sending them to Mr Rundell simply to stop him starting a search for her. Mr Rundell, did you ever say anything to Dr Gair to make him afraid you might do that?'

Hugh did not answer for a moment. He seemed to be groping clumsily in his memory and finding only confusion. Then he nodded.

'Yes, I remember I told Charles I was thinking of divorcing her and that I meant to find out where she was. I think I said I was thinking of hiring a private detective to look for her. He didn't discourage me. He seemed to think it was a good idea.'

'But soon after that a letter came?'

'Yes.'

'It was from Rome,' Isobel said. 'And it more or less said she wanted to come back to us. And for weeks and weeks I kept expecting her, but she didn't come.'

'And seeing how much it meant to Isobel, you see,' Hugh said, 'I thought, if my wife wanted to come back, I'd let her. So I did nothing more about the private detective.'

'And do you remember if Dr Gair was away when that letter came?' Patrick asked. 'Or had he been away just before it?'

'I don't remember – yes – no – no, I really don't remember. But he was away for a few days last week, just before the last letter came from Paris.'

'And he was away when the letter came from Mexico,' Valerie said. 'I remember that distinctly. Mr Rundell brought it to show us, and afterwards – I don't know why I remember this, but I just do – my brother and I took the dogs for a walk and while we were out we talked about the letters and how much better it would be for everyone if Debbie would stop writing, upsetting Hugh and Isobel every time. And of course, if we were looking after the dogs, it means Dr Gair was away. But I think we just thought he was in London.'

'Mexico!' Alberti Barragan exclaimed. 'Now at last we get to Mexico! Where does my father fit into this story? You have suggested he was having an affair with Mrs Rundell. I have told you this was impossible. Now you know it was impossible. She was never in Mexico. She was dead. So why did this man, Charles Gair, murder my father?'

'I think your father became quite unconsciously what Dr Gair thought was a danger to him,' Patrick said. 'Perhaps we'll never know the exact truth of what happened, but I think it was something like this. Dr Barragan and Dr Gair met somewhere in Mexico. The meeting was of no importance. Perhaps they met in a bar or a restaurant and talked about the weather or the antiquities of Mexico. But then Dr Barragan came to England and by a fearful misfortune, on his very first evening in London, he came face to face with Dr Gair, probably in the entrance to Neville's restaurant, where Dr Gair was in the habit of going. And he panicked, because if Dr Barragan should meet anyone else who knew Gair – and he was a fairly well-known man in certain circles, wasn't he, a Fellow of the Royal Society and all that? – well, if Dr Barragan had met anyone who'd known Gair, he would have talked in all innocence about their encounter in Mexico. And that might have got round to Mr Rundell, who'd just had a letter from Mexico, and he could have been a little too impressed by the coincidence of that letter coming and Gair's visit there. So Gair took Dr Barragan to some restaurant where he wasn't known, then invited him for a drive through London at night, and some time on that drive, in the darkness, he killed him, brought him home here and put him in his cupboard. I believe that's what happened, but as I said, I don't think we'll ever be a hundred per cent sure.'

'Yes,' Alberti Barragan said. 'Yes, it could have been so.'

'Gair was an artist, of course,' Patrick added, 'and generally clever with his hands. It could have been easier for him than for most people to produce a tolerable forgery of Mrs Rundell's writing. And from what I've heard of him, it wouldn't surprise me if it gave him a perverted sort of pleasure to compose the letters in Mrs Rundell's style and watch their effect.'

Hugh brushed a hand across his forehead. 'But why did he kill Debbie?' he demanded. 'Why Debbie? She was in love with him. She left me because of him. Of course, I always knew that. Then I knew things must have come to an end between them, because she went away. Perhaps it was something to do with his career, I thought, or perhaps he'd been stringing her along all the time, letting her think he'd break up his marriage for her. But now you say he killed her.'

'I don't think I actually did say that,' Patrick said.

'You did, you said ...' Hugh paused, frowning with heavy concentration. 'What do you mean?' he asked.

'I think all I said was that I'd worked out by a more or less logical process that there ought to be a body under the rockery, and that I'd thought the body would be Mrs Gair's until she walked in alive and well. And I said that the evidence of the jewellery makes it seem probable that the body we've found is your wife's. And I've said that the letters which made you think she was alive were forgeries, probably sent to you by Dr Gair, to stop you starting a real search for her. But I haven't said he killed her.'

'But who else ... ?' Hugh began and paused again, knuckling his forehead. There were beads of sweat on it.

'I didn't mention,' Patrick said, 'that Dr Gair buried something along with Mrs Rundell's body. A knife, very carefully wrapped up in plastic, which hasn't decayed with the years. A common kitchen knife, very sharp, which we think was used to stab Mrs Rundell. And it still has the fingerprints of the killer on it, prints that at a first examination look remarkably like those, Mrs Gair, that you left on the silver cigarette box on the piano in your sitting-room a little while ago.'

Rhona drew in a whistling breath. She jerked suddenly forward to the edge of her chair and crouched there, almost as if she had cramp in her stomach. Her face was ugly with strain.

After a moment she whispered harshly, 'I'm not going to say anything.'

'That's your right,' Patrick said. 'But I must ask you to accompany Sergeant Farley and myself to the police station, and it is my duty to warn you that you are not obliged to say anything, but that anything you say will be taken down in writing and may be used in evidence.' He looked round the room. 'You see, Charles Gair was not unprepared to help his wife when she killed Deborah Rundell in a fit of jealous rage. To some degree he may have blamed himself for what had happened. So he sent his wife away to London, telling her, I think, that the price of his help was that she should get out of his life and stay out. Then he concealed the body. But he never meant to be convicted of murder himself. In case the body of Deborah Rundell should ever be found, the evidence against his wife was buried along with it. And it was in the hope of stopping its being found, of the rockery being touched, that you came here today, wasn't it, Mrs Gair?'

Still crouching on the edge of her chair, like an animal hypnotized into rigidity by fear, Rhona began to mutter inaudibly to herself. Hugh looked at her with a flame of hatred in his eyes that brought unusual life to his stunned face.

Patrick turned to him. 'Mr Rundell, I must ask you to accompany us too. Even if you didn't know it before, something about that last letter from Paris told you that all the earlier letters had been forgeries. You guessed your wife had been dead for years and that Gair had killed her. So you let your daughter have the car and sent her out for the evening, as you thought, with Dr Haydon, and you came here on foot, believing that Dr Hackett and Mrs Bayne would be out at a meeting and that no one would see you. And you killed Gair, then tried to make his death look like suicide by hanging him from the beam. And you took his passport because it gave away the secrets of his travels, which might be connected up, as you'd connected it up, with the forged letters and so reveal your motive. And you left and walked home.'

'Oh no!' Isobel cried out. 'It can't be! Daddy, it isn't true! They can't take you!'

Hearing her, Hugh need have had no more fears that his daughter did not love him. He gave her a smile as he stood up.

'I'll come with you,' he said to Patrick in a tone of extreme weariness. 'Valerie, will you look after Isobel till things get sorted out?'

'Mrs Gair,' Patrick said, then, as she rose, he turned back to Hugh and delivered the same words of the official warning as he had to Rhona.

Chapter 19

Isobel refused to stay with Edmund and Valerie. She said that she was going straight into Keyfield to see her father's solicitor. Neither of them tried to argue with her. She left with Ivor Haydon and Alberti Barragan.

When they had all gone and there was no one left in the room but herself and Edmund, Valerie absent-mindedly poured out some of the cold coffee that no one had touched, started to drink it, grimaced and put the cup down. Edmund began to wander about the room. Valerie's eyes followed him as he moved from one end of it to the other. There was no sound in the room but that of his pacing footsteps. After all the voices, all the talking, the place seemed hollow, a place in which perhaps nothing would ever be heard again, except for muted echoes.

After some minutes Valerie asked, 'What are you going to do?'

'There's only one thing I can do, isn't there?' he said. 'I almost did it at once, before they took him away. Now I wish I had. It might have been easier than doing it in cold blood. I'm scared, Val, I'm very scared.'

'I'm scared too,' she said.

'I'd like to find a good argument for doing nothing.'

'What did you do with the passport?'

He stood still, put a hand in his breast pocket and brought out his wallet, took a passport out of it and handed it to Valerie.

'Why did you take it?' she asked.

'It was automatic,' he said. 'I was holding it, looking at it, when Charles came in and found me and I just jammed it into my pocket. And afterwards, when I was cleaning my fingerprints off the writing table and everything else I could remember having touched, it occurred to me I couldn't be sure I could get the fingerprints off the cover of the passport. I didn't know how effective plain rubbing would be on the cardboard of the cover.'

'And you just kept it in your pocket!' Valerie said. 'Isn't that just like you? Why didn't you destroy it?'

'I suppose I thought it might be needed as evidence if someone else got arrested for Charles's murder.'

'But it wasn't really murder, was it? You killed him, but it wasn't murder.'

'I hardly know, isn't that strange?' he said. 'At the time it felt like an accident. He was coming at me with the poker, I defended myself, he fell and cracked his skull on the fender and he died. But then something happened to me ... Valerie, can you murder a man after he's dead?'

'Of course not.'

'But if it's what you've got inside you. All that hatred.' He looked intently into her face. 'Since when have you known all this?'

'Perhaps since you took down Charles's picture. No, it wasn't then. It was since Sunday evening, when we took the dogs for a walk. Well, that's when I began to think about it.'

'Why?'

'You'd just told me you'd heard from Ruth Isaacs that I hadn't been at the Botanical Society meeting and you asked me if I'd been the person you'd seen coming away from Charles's door. I reminded you I'd been wearing my red suit and you said you'd forgotten what I was wearing. But still, I thought, if it had been me, you'd have recognized me. You don't have to see a person clearly to recognize someone you know well. And then somehow I started thinking, suppose you hadn't seen the person at all, but only heard them. Heard them knocking at Charles's door while you were *inside* the house and didn't dare look out. And once you knew I hadn't been at the meeting, you had to find out if the person was me, because if it was it probably meant I'd gone home afterwards and found you weren't there. Yes, that's how I began to think about it.'

'And that was all?'

'No, there was another thing we talked about on that walk. We talked about the way you'd lost all interest in women in the last few years, although you hadn't been like that when you were younger. Then just now, when I heard it was Debbie they'd found buried, I guessed you'd somehow found that out and that that was why you killed Charles, because you'd been in love with Debbie yourself and nobody else has meant anything to you since she died. But I don't know how you found out she was dead.'

'Much in the same way as your detective friend did,' he said. 'It came out of having the sort of mind I have. I suppose it's what got me as far as I managed to get in science. I notice discrepancies and coincidences. I'm inclined to believe they may mean something. And it happened to occur to me that Debbie's letters always came when Charles was away. Then there was the queerness of the letters themselves. There was something unreal about them. The more I thought about them, the less convincing they seemed. And then one day it suddenly hit me that it was Charles who was writing and posting them.'

He had begun to pace the room again.

'You can get haunted by an idea, even one as tenuous as that, you know. You can't get it out of your mind. The feeling that I had to know if I was right grew and grew on me. I thought if I could get a look at Charles's passport, that would be a first step in checking whether he'd really travelled to the places the letters had come from. But you were one of my problems. I didn't want you to know anything about the sort of things I had on my mind, or that I meant to get into the house and look for the passport when Charles was out of the house. I tried to find an opportunity last week, when he was away, but you always seemed to appear at an inconvenient moment. So I had the idea of going sick on Saturday, when I knew you'd be going out for the evening and Charles would be taking the dogs for their usual walk. I told you I was feeling ill

165

and thought I'd caught the bug that was going around and wouldn't be going to the meeting, and when you'd left and I'd seen Charles start out with the dogs I cut across to the house and started my hunt for the passport. What I didn't know was that Charles was only going out for a little while, because he was expecting Isobel, and he came back just as I'd found the passport and was standing there, holding it. He came into the room, shutting the door behind him with the dogs outside before he saw me, and then . . .'

He paused at the window, gripping the sill with both hands and staring out at the other house. When he went on his voice had gone suddenly hoarse.

'When he saw me, when I saw his face, I knew beyond all doubt that I was right. He saw me there, holding the passport open. He made a sort of noise. I can't describe it. Then he snatched up the poker and came at me. I can't tell you what happened next. I don't know much about fighting. I was just trying to defend myself. And then there he was, lying at my feet, dead. I don't remember much about the next few minutes. No, it was more than a few minutes. I just stood there, doing nothing. Then I saw Charles's bunch of keys on the floor. He'd let himself into the house with them and when he saw me he just dropped them. I don't know what made me think of the cupboard in the cellar then. I suppose I'd always felt there was a mystery about it, with that padlock on it. It was the only thing in the house that was carefully locked up. So with the feeling I had then that the whole of Charles's life had been a mystery, I thought I'd investigate that little bit of it. And I found Barragan. And my mind worked like Dunn's. I understood what had happened to Debbie. The whole thing hit me all at once as if it was deadly simple. I know I was insane for a time then. I'd killed Charles in self-defence, I hadn't murdered him, but at that point I became a murderer, I hanged him.'

'So hanging him had nothing to do with trying to make his death look like suicide,' Valerie said. 'That's why you didn't even bother to put a chair near his feet.'

'It was an execution!' Edmund cried. 'I didn't even think just then of trying to conceal the meaning of what I'd done.'

'Then Isobel came and knocked.'

'Yes, and went on and on. And on and on. She couldn't believe Charles had forgotten her. She didn't give up easily.'

'What did you do then?'

'Cleaned up the fingerprints and came home. And then I really started being sick. There was no faking about what happened that night. I was sick over and over again.'

He turned away from the window to face her once more, but he seemed to have nothing more to say. There was a chilly silence in the room that suddenly made Valerie shiver.

'Perhaps you won't get into really serious trouble if you tell the police the story you've just told me,' she said.

'I don't care much what trouble I get into,' he answered. 'Nothing seems to matter much.'

'When are you going in to them?'

'Now, I suppose. There's no point in putting it off. I wonder if your policeman friend will be surprised or if he's waiting for me to do it?'

'Why d'you keep calling him my friend?' she asked.

'Because I've seen him looking at you. He isn't a man who gives his feelings away much, but he hasn't even tried to hide what they are about you.'

She shook her head slightly, but knew that there was a certain dishonesty in it, and that in this short time that she and Edmund still had together it was a time for truthfulness only.

'I suppose it was because you felt all along that you'd give yourself up sooner or later that made you encourage me to go away and get back to work,' she said. 'You were always against it when I talked about it earlier.'

'Yes, I didn't think I was anything much for you to go on holding on to,' he answered. 'The sooner you could manage on your own, the better.'

She stood up. 'If you're going now, I'll go with you.'

'No,' he said quickly.

'Yes.'

'No, my dear, this is something I'm going to do by myself,' he said quietly. 'I've leant on you far more than I should have during these past years. But we were both bereft, weren't we, you of Michael, I of Debbie? So we had a lot to give one another and it worked very well. And for all you've given me, I'm very grateful. But now we're going different ways and starting now, I'm going on my own. I'll take the car and if they keep me at the police station, as I suppose they will, you'll be able to pick it up later this evening. So good-bye, Val, and don't worry too much about what happens to me. I'm not worrying myself any more, now that I've told you everything. I really don't mind what happens.'

She came to him quickly and put her arms round him. They kissed, a thing which they had never been in the habit of doing. Then he put her away from him, walked straight to the door and out into the afternoon sunshine. From the open door Valerie watched him walking away. She wanted to call out to him before he reached the car, but she knew that he did not want to look round again. She stood there until she had heard the car, then she turned slowly back into the room and shut the door behind her.

She was never sure afterwards how she got through the rest of the afternoon. She spent a good deal of the time simply sitting in a chair, doing nothing. She thought a good deal of Michael and of the first day or two that she had lived through after his death. She thought of things that she and Edmund had done together, not only in the last few years, but long ago in their childhoods. She did not think at all about the future, her own or his. Time had run up against a blank wall, too high for there to be any point in trying to look over it.

She was aware of growing stiff in the chair, of changing her position and settling into a new one, only to grow stiff again and have to move once more. The dogs lay on the hearthrug near her. She thought of some odd jobs about the house that she might do to pass the time, but when she stood up, vaguely meaning to get started on one, a heavy lethargy possessed her, making her sink back into the chair again, lean back, yawn and almost fall asleep. Yet as soon as she closed her eyes her mind became violently active, with images of nightmare choking her imagination. The waking stupor was preferable.

It was the dogs that startled her out of it. Both suddenly sat up at the same time, uttering deep, warning growls. A moment later there was a knock at the door. Getting up, the dogs went prowling towards it. But when Valerie pulled herself out of the chair, followed them, opened the door and found Patrick Dunn standing there, they decided to welcome him, wagging their tails and giving his hands a few friendly licks. He stood there looking unusually unsure of himself.

'May I come in?' he asked, not in his policeman's voice, but in a tone that Valerie had not heard from him before, different, rather humble.

She stood aside for him to enter, called the dogs in again and shut the door.

He looked round curiously, as if he had never been in the room before. He might have been seeing it for the first time not as a place where witnesses had to be questioned, but as one where people lived their lives.

'You're all alone here,' he said after a little pause.

'Yes,' Valerie answered, then added, 'Please sit down.'

They both sat down, facing one another, in chairs on either side of the fireplace. The dogs settled down on the hearthrug again.

'Haven't you some friend who could come in for the night?' Patrick asked. 'Or isn't there someone you could go to?'

'I'd sooner be alone,' she said.

'I wish you weren't.'

'There are times when it's best to be alone,' she answered.

'But it's pretty solitary out here now.'

'I've never worried about that. Anyway, I've got the dogs. I'll be quite all right.'

'I wasn't really thinking of that. I was thinking of what one's mind can sometimes start doing to one when there's no one around.'

She looked at him curiously. She already knew that there was something between them that had nothing to do with his work and the pain that he had had to inflict on her, and the thought of it scared her, because there was something in him that reminded her of Michael, and although that might stir her strongly, it was not a promise of peace of mind.

It took her by surprise, however, when he went on, 'Mrs Bayne, do you hate me?'

'Hate you? Why should I?' she asked.

'We'll have to charge him, you know.'

'With murder?'

'Yes.'

Her heart gave a lurch, but she answered calmly, 'You've only been doing your job.'

'We may manage to get the charge reduced to manslaughter.'

'*You* may manage ... ? Do you want to?'

'If his story's true, you see, it wasn't murder,' he said. 'If it can be proved that Gair attacked him and that he fought Gair off in self-defence and killed him accidentally, well, that isn't murder. But if your brother attacked Gair first and it was Gair who was defending himself, that *is* murder.'

'And how do you believe it happened?' she asked.

'I want to believe your brother,' he answered. 'And I think a jury will. They're going to be on his side once the facts about Gair's character come out.'

'Tell me,' she said, 'did you guess it was Edmund when you arrested Hugh Rundell?'

'We didn't arrest him, you know. We were only asking him to help us with our inquiries. We never got as far as charging him.'

'But when you did that, were you expecting it would make my brother confess?'

'Let's say I thought it was a possibility. At first I wrote him off as a suspect, although he'd keys to the house and had managed to get rid of you by saying he was too ill to go out, because I didn't think he'd be so ignorant as to try to fake a suicide like that. But then a talk I had with Haydon and Barragan about hanging reminded me that it can be execution as well as suicide. It made me think Barragan might have done it if there was any way he could have found out about his father's death. He's violent and vengeful enough, I thought. But I'd picked up some gossip from Mrs Fullerton about your brother and Deborah Rundell, so when we found her body I could think of a motive for your brother. But no, I won't say I was sure what had happened. I'm not omniscient.'

'When can I see him?' Valerie asked.

'Tomorrow, if you like. But first I'd see his solicitor. There's his defence to think about.'

'Yes, of course.'

After that they were both silent. Neither of them was a person who could advance quickly into intimacy, though something in each was trying to find words in which to express some kindness, some warmth, some understanding of the problems that troubled them both.

Patrick was the first to find a few words, inadequate yet urgently spoken. 'And remember, I'm not your enemy.'

'I've never felt you were,' she answered.

'And when you go to London – well, it isn't a world away. If I can help . . .'

'I don't know if I'll be going now,' she said. 'I'll have things to see to here.'

'But you'll go in the end.'

Unless, he suddenly found himself adding in his own mind, I can stop you.

And it seemed to him, not quite reasonably yet with astonishing certainty, that the brief smile that lightened Valerie's stricken face just then was in answer to that thought of his, rather than to what he had said to her.

More about Penguins
and Pelicans

Penguinews, which appears every month, contains details of all the new books issued by Penguins as they are published. From time to time it is supplemented by *Penguins in Print*, which is our complete list of almost 5,000 titles.

A specimen copy of *Penguinews* will be sent to you free on request. Please write to Dept EP, Penguin Books Ltd, Harmondsworth, Middlesex, for your copy.

In the U.S.A.: For a complete list of books available from Penguins in the United States write to Dept CS, Penguin Books, 625 Madison Avenue, New York, New York 10022.

In Canada: For a complete list of books available from Penguins in Canada write to Penguin Books Canada Ltd, 2801 John Street, Markham, Ontario L3R 1B4.

Michael Innes

An Awkward Lie

'Mr Appleby,' Sergeant Howard remarks, 'you seem to be in rather an awkward lie.'

For Bobby – Sir John Appleby's engaging son – is having a hard time proving his case. He did see a corpse on the golf course. And a very attractive girl did appear on the scene. But by the time he had telephoned for the police and returned, there was no girl, and no corpse . . .

Also published in Penguins:

From *London* Far
Hamlet, Revenge!
Money from Holme
What Happened at Hazelwood

Patricia Moyes

The Curious Affair of the Third Dog

' "Poor Henry." Jane sounded amused. "Well, we've got a perfectly riveting mystery for you right here in the village."

"No," said Henry firmly.

"The Case of The Third Dog!" said Jane dramatically.

"The what?"

"Mystery Hound Vanishes Without Trace. Is International Gang Involved?" "Well, is it?" His eyes shut.

Henry leant further back in his chair and turned his face to catch the last rays of the sun.

"That's for the Wizard of the Yard to find out," said Jane.'